HAPPILY EVER AFTER

HAPPILY EVER AFTER

MELANIE MARTINS

Melanie Martins

BOOK TWO

BLOSSOM IN WINTER V

Melanie Martins, LLC
www.blossominwinter.com

First published in the United States by Melanie Martins, LLC in 2021.

ISBSN ebook 979-8-9852380-5-1

ISBN Paperback 979-8-9852380-1-3

Printed and bound in Great Britain by Clays Ltd, Elcograf S.p.A

This is a 1st Edition.

DISCLAIMER

This novel is a work of fiction written in American-English and is intended for mature audiences. Names, characters, places, and incidents are either the product of the author's imagination or used fictitiously. Any resemblance to actual persons, living or dead, is entirely coincidental. This novel contains strong and explicit language, graphic sexuality, and other sensitive content that may be disturbing for some readers.

To all of you, my dear readers.
Thank you.

CHAPTER 1

Manhattan, December 19, 2021
Petra Van Gatt

"What's wrong?" Alex asks in the most innocent voice I have ever heard as he cautiously walks towards me. Despite his question, I'm pretty sure he knows *exactly* what's wrong.

I can barely contain my anger, but I make an effort to extend my hand and show him the screen of my phone that displays his mother's message.

My husband narrows his eyes, focusing on her SMS. "Oh, jeez!" He blows out a breath, running a hand through his wet hair. "I never thought she'd do that. I swear."

My brows raise up instantly in confusion. "Do what?"

"Send you a text like that," he answers. "I'm so sorry."

The text doesn't matter for god's sake, I want to say out loud, but instead, and keeping my tone low so as to not wake up the twins, I ask, "But is it true or not that she is spending Christmas with us?"

"She was gonna spend it all alone Petra…"

I can't help rolling my eyes, unable to give a damn about it.

"All of my sisters are spending Christmas abroad this year."

As if it makes any difference!

"Yara is in Paris, Julia in a safari with her family somewhere in Kenya, and Maud will be in Germany. They nearly begged me to take her."

I shake my head, so freaking disappointed at him for not standing his ground. "You could have said no."

"She's still my mother, Petra."

"But she killed mine!" I scream in a whisper.

We see the twins moving slightly in their carriers, most likely disturbed at the strange noises coming from us, so we remain silent for a few seconds, while I try to calm down.

"The thing is, it's not just my mom who is joining us," he ventures cautiously.

"What do you mean?" I ask, already worried someone else from his family is coming over.

"Your dad and Catherine might have also invited themselves along."

I let out a breath in exasperation at the news, dropping my arms against my hips. I purse my lips tight in a failed attempt to chill. Well, our first Christmas together and Alex managed to ruin it. "Why would you invite them?"

"Your dad wanted to invite us over and I told him we couldn't as we were going to Aspen and he just… invited himself," he says, keeping his tone so low that I can barely understand everything. "What could I do? Besides, he booked a villa for himself and Catherine, so it's not like they are staying with us."

As I ponder his explanation, having Dad and his girlfriend in Aspen is not *that* problematic—after all, I know Dad enjoys his privacy and is not a pain in the ass like Margaret is. "That's not an excuse to bring your mother too."

"Look, she will be there just for four nights. That's it. She flies back to the Netherlands right after Christmas," he answers as he starts drying himself with the towel. "It's not the end of the world."

It might not be the end of the world for him, but having to spend Christmas with the woman responsible for my mother's death was the last thing I wanted to do.

***

The drive home is the tensest thirty minutes I have experienced in weeks, and I think the twins can sense it too. They fuss quietly in the back seat, clearly feeling some of the unrest flowing between their parents.

I'm dumbfounded still. Christmas with Margaret? Of all people. What have I done over the past few months to make Alex think that this is something I would ever be okay with? I waffle between being pissed off and on the verge of tears, feeling like my holiday is entirely ruined.

"You're going to have to stop pouting," Alex tells me, his jaw clenched and staring straight ahead.

I cross my arms and ignore him, staring resolutely out the window at the city as it passes. Damn it, I had plans! A calm, gentle Christmas with my family. I deserve the whole cheesy Christmas experience after everything I have been through this year, but no, Margaret has to stick her nose where it doesn't belong and ruin everything. As always.

"You were excited about Aspen and totally fine with your dad being there," Alex tries to speak to me again, taking a different tactic. "Isn't that a bit hypocritical?"

I can't hold my tongue any longer. "You like my dad!" I snap. "It's different. For fuck's sake, Alex!"

"It isn't," Alex says tightly. "But whatever you need to tell yourself, Petra."

I'm so angry that I can hear my pulse in my ears, the blood rushing in my head. I take a few deep breaths, trying to lower the tension inside of me before we get home, and everyone knows that we've been fighting.

We drive in silence for the majority of the rest of the trip, Alex tries to goad me into talking a few more times, to no avail. I refuse to fight in front of the kids, so I bite the inside of my cheek until we finally get home.

I can feel the situation starting to heat up again as we unlatch the car seats from their bases and head to the lift. The twins are fighting sleep, and I can't help but think they aren't fully taking a nap because the almost fight between their parents has them grouchy.

We enter the condo and silently unbuckle the babies. I know that my refusal to talk is eating away at Alex, but I haven't really had time to digest the news. It had been like whiplash, to go from joy at spending Christmas in Aspen with Alex and the babies, to the despair of knowing that Alex's mother would be joining us. Not to mention the more subtle blow of learning my dad and his new girlfriend would be coming too. I felt like I had only a scant few weeks of peace with my children, and now I'm being thrown right back to the wolves.

As much as Alex is the love of my life, the underhanded manipulation that comes along with his social and family circles are exactly what I had wanted to escape when I was a little girl. No one ever seems to behave like a real person around Alex and me, besides the ones closest to us. Instead, everyone wears a fake face. Cleverly decorated masks that they all use to stab us in the back when we least expect it. It's exhausting and his mom is a perfect example of such.

Jasmine clings to the collar of my shirt, her little fists tight, and nuzzles her face into my collarbone. It eases some of the anger burning inside me, and I return her snuggle, placing a kiss on her downy-soft hair. She sighs heavily, relaxing against me. Yeah, she's really sleepy, poor thing.

Alex lifts Jasper out of his carrier, and I can see our son is equally tuckered out. Alex opens his mouth to speak, but I hold up a finger of my free hand to my lips, telling him to hush. His expression turns pinched and annoyed, but now just isn't the time. I honestly just needed some time to think.

I know… I'll go up to the atelier and paint my feelings out. There is a certain quietness in my mind when I paint that makes it the perfect activity to sort through tough thoughts and decisions. First, I have to ditch Alex. I can tell he's brimming with unsaid words.

I brush past him, Jasmine still nodding off in my arms, and nearly run into Lily. She greets me with a polite smile.

"Welcome home, everyone. How did the little mermaids do at—oh." She pauses, looking from my face to Alex's, and she reads between the lines, sensing the brewing argument.

Lily reaches forward and gently takes the snoozing Jasmine from my grip, her words coming out more carefully this time. "I'm going to go put Jasmine down for her nap. Alex, I'll be right back for Jasper."

He gives her a curt nod, and she looks at me questioningly. I shake my head quickly, and she takes the hint, carrying Jasmine to the nursery. I follow behind her and then take the next set of stairs to the atelier, knowing that Alex must be internally fuming at my retreat, but hopefully he'll take the hint and leave me alone for a little while.

The smell of paint and turpentine washes over me as I open the door to the atelier, and it immediately relaxes me. My little bit of sanctuary. I shut the door behind me, and stand in the open room for a moment, soaking it all in.

The hazy winter lights illuminate the room through the enormous windows, with lazy snowflakes falling sporadically over the city. None of them stick around long, but they are a forewarning of the winter to come. We can't hide from the impending snowstorms forever.

The building is much draftier up here, and I rub my hands together as I gather my supplies, not having any sort of painting in mind, but just going with the flow. I grab grays and blues and a single evergreen, depositing them on the lip of my easel before setting a medium-sized canvas in front of them. I gaze out at the city, but instead, I see the mountains of Colorado. Okay, well, if I've got mountains on the brain, I'll paint mountains too.

I start to paint and let my thoughts wander. The trip is problematic, and if I put my foot down, I'm sure I can avoid going, but it will upset Alex if I refuse. After the tumultuous year we've had, I've tried to avoid fighting with him when possible, and this is the biggest scuffle we've had in so long. Honestly, it leaves me a bit shaken. I don't enjoy thinking about all the other fights we've had.

I sketch my mountains out with a dull pencil and chew absentmindedly on the eraser, as I think. How much does escaping this awful vacation mean to me? Would I be having Christmas alone, which would also mean that Alex would be away from his children during their first Christmas? I frown. No, that would never happen. So either he'd stay and be miserable or I'd go and be equally miserable.

Both of those options suck. Spreading the first dollop of paint on the canvas, I work it in. Can I tolerate Margaret? After all, the vacation is only a few days long, and from what Alex says, she is just desperate to spend time with her grandchildren and son, given the fact she hasn't seen us since the twins' baptism. Plus he claims that she'll only be there until the day after Christmas Day… but who's to say she won't find a way to stick around longer?

Is Alex actually fooled by her act? I thought that he and I were on the same page regarding his snake of a mother, but I guess not. I toss the brush I'm using in the jar of water next to me, but before I can pick up the next brush, the door to the atelier creaks open.

Alex has apparently changed into jeans and a fitted black t-shirt, his hair wet all over again. Either the shower at the swim school hadn't cut it for him, or he'd also needed some alone time to think. His feet are bare on the wooden floor, and if we hadn't been in the middle of a disagreement, I'd have found him ridiculously handsome in this soft, domestic form.

"How long are you going to keep avoiding me?" he asks, leaning against the doorframe.

"It's only been like an hour," I reply, snatching a new brush up and continuing to paint. I can't stand sitting here under his watchful eyes without keeping busy. This topic makes me nervous.

"An hour too long," he replies, his tone neutral. At least he seems to have chilled out a bit.

I keep painting, but as the seconds stretch on I blow out a breath and respond. "I don't know what you want me to say exactly. I hate the idea of being anywhere near your mom. I hate her holding my children and pretending that everything is fine. Sorry to say, but with the exception of your dad, I don't have any interest in being around your family."

He closes his eyes for a second. "I thought you'd realize by now that it's not as simple as that. I came with some baggage, and that includes my family." His face takes on a guarded look. "Are you regretting taking on that baggage, Petra?"

"Never," I say meekly.

He seems momentarily relieved. "Petra, we're going to Aspen."

I rub my hands over my face, hoping that I'm not smearing paint all over myself. "I know."

"Can't you find even a little bit of excitement about this? We're spending Christmas exactly where I took you two years ago. We're going back to our *winter wonderland*." He puts amused inflection on the last two words, but it doesn't drag the smile out of me he's expecting.

Although... I appreciate how calmly he's approaching this problem. When I saw the look on his face in the car, I was sure I was going to see some of the cold and calculated Alex that comes out when he really needs to win an argument at work. When we had first gotten together, Alex had used that cutting edge of his personality to win disagreements between us, too. I don't love the cajoling, but at least he's trying.

"Petra," he sighs. "Can you at least look at me?"

I set my brush down and turn to face him, our eyes meeting. He holds my gaze, and the space between us seems both miles long and mere inches. Neither of us speaks for the moment, and I hope he can see in my gaze the turmoil that I'm going through. Alex seems to explore my eyes for a few moments, and I sort of wish that I had something to say to end the argument, but there was nothing new to add. Alex knows I don't want to see or be around his mom, and he also knows how important this Christmas is to me. What else is there to say, knowing he's going to get his way and I'm going to be left with no choice? Left empty handed.

I pinch the bridge of my nose and sigh. "I'm done talking about this for right now."

He barks a laugh, incredulous. "Done? We haven't even really started. You just want to pout and paint and ignore me."

I bristle at that, and in a fit of making a point, I stand and turn my easel and chair away from him, continuing to paint with my back towards him. I can almost feel Alex stewing behind me, and if I could see him, I know that he'd be clenching and unclenching his fists in frustration.

I expect another cutting remark, or maybe that he'll just turn around and leave. What I don't expect is Alex's swift footsteps behind me, and then suddenly he's there, one hand clamped on the back of my neck while he growls into my ear. "You will not ignore me like this, little Petra."

I gasp when he fastens his teeth on the shell of my ear, the brush clattering to the floor. He moves his hand from my nape to my shoulder, thumb brushing against my pulse point. The heat of his anger has transformed into another sort of heat, and if we weren't going to work through our issues with words, apparently we were going to work through them another way.

I try to turn to face him, but he holds me fast, a hand on each of my shoulders now, as he nips and kisses at the back of my neck, his breath hot on my chilled skin.

"Alex," I breathe, and he chuckles sarcastically.

"Oh, so now you're speaking to me. Stand up."

Gulping, I do as I'm told. Alex doesn't even bother to shut the door of the atelier or the curtains over the windows that face out into the city as he pulls my soft cashmere sweater over my head. I hadn't bothered putting on anything underneath after the class, figuring I'd have a long hot shower and change once I got home. Now I stand shivering in the drafty room only in jeans, my bare toes curling over the old wooden floors.

Alex moves so that he is now in front of me, undoing the button of my jeans as his eyes sweep over my body, taking in how my nipples have pebbled in the chill and the goosebumps rising on my flesh. He works at the zipper of my pants as he leans in, kissing me briefly.

"Have I got your attention now?" he asks in a low growl, pinching one nipple and causing me to cry out. For some reason, I hold my tongue and the dark laugh he gives me makes me momentarily wary.

"I said," he starts, tugging my pants to the floor and pulling me forward so I stumble out of them. "Have I got your attention?"

I turn my jaw away, both flushed with the heat of his touch while still being mildly annoyed that he is blindsiding me by turning my very real feelings into a sex game, but any of my rational thoughts are thrown out the window when he cups my pussy over my white cotton panties, sliding a finger down my covered slit. I don't know if it was the adrenaline of having Alex undress me here, or how turned on his domineering side always makes me, but I'm already soaking wet for him.

"Answer me," he demands, yanking my panties down too so I'm completely bare before him. "Or I leave you up here, alone. And nude."

"Yes," I bite out, swaying into his touch when he rewards my reluctant answer by pulling me into his embrace. "Yes, you have my attention."

"Good," he tells me shortly, and he gives me a minute to snuggle my naked form into him, absorbing his warmth, before he slips his arm under my bottom and hoists me up. I instinctually wrap my legs around him as he carries me to the enormous windows, cloudy with frost, and before I can muster a squeal, he has pressed my bare back to the glass.

I suck in air, shocked at the sudden, nearly unbearable chill, and try to squirm away. Alex supports me with one arm, keeping me pinned to the glass as he works at his own jeans until they fall to his ankles.

The only source of warmth for me is the hot press of his unclothed hips and erect shaft crowding against my thighs. I'm full-on shaking now, both from the cold and the thrill of what we're about to do. As he wordlessly fits himself at my entrance, I dazedly realize he hadn't been wearing underwear. That prick, he had been planning this all along!

My treacherous mind goes blank when he pushes himself inside, through my damp folds, and straight to my core. A small whine escapes my lips, while Alex presses his forehead to mine with a drawn-out groan.

"You win," I pant, stopping my struggles and wrapping my legs tight around him. His huff stirs the loose hair at my neck, and after he lets us both adjust for a few seconds, he begins to move.

I'm freezing when he starts, but within minutes I'm hot all over, the heat of our bodies clearing the fog from the windows. Alex cups my chin with one hand, supporting my weight with his body and my arms around his shoulders. "Look at me," he says, his voice leaving no room for argument.

I lift my eyes to his, feeling dazed as he drives into me over and over. Satisfaction and triumph flash over his expression, and he kisses me bruisingly before pulling back. "Keep your eyes on me the whole time. Don't hide from me, wife. Stay with me."

Oh. This isn't just about the sex or the argument. Was Alex… afraid that I was shutting him out? That had never been my intention. He watches my face, my eyes, the curve of my throat as I throw my head back, tension building inside me like an oncoming storm.

"Stay with me," Alex repeats, his own voice fraught with how close he was to finishing.

"Always," I whimper. "I'm so close, Alex."

He tilts his hips, just so, and the thick head of his manhood strokes my inner walls in such a way that suddenly I'm having trouble breathing. "Just like that," I encourage. "I'm going to… I'm g—"

The back of my head hits the glass with a "thunk" as lightning shoots down my spine and I come undone around Alex's cock. He curses, clutching me harder as he thrusts into me erratically before he too is coming apart at the seams.

My peak rushes over me in waves as Alex stays pressed against me, and for a time I'm not sure where he begins and I end. As I come back to my senses, the cold seeps in from my back again, and I feel his body start to relax in small increments.

Still, I don't fight him or protest as he takes my lips in an achingly tender kiss, telling me without words that he needs me, and not to shut him out again. I let my fingers tangle through his hair, and in the back of my mind, I vaguely think, *Fine, Aspen it is.*

Alex and I dress quietly, having said so much of what needed to be said with our bodies. My insecurities are still rolling inside me like the tides, but there is nothing to do about it now. I hadn't even seen Margaret yet, and here she was driving a wedge between Alex and me. We needed to get ahead of that negativity, and the sooner the better.

He kisses my forehead gently, and we walk downstairs, leaving my half-painted mountain scape behind. There's a lot to do, so I decide that I can just pick things up later again.

Back on the first floor, I make my way to the shower while Alex goes to his office to get some work done. I try not to think about the insane amount of packing that will have to be done for myself and the twins as I shower, letting the hot water pour over me and wash away at least some of my worries.

Scrubbing my hair between my hands, I mentally take stock of my biggest concerns so I can deal with them first. There was no ditching Margaret. She was undoubtedly coming with us, but that didn't mean we had to spend all our time with her. I make a mental note to check out all the family friendly activities in the area to keep us busy and away from his mother.

Since Margaret is only staying with us for four nights, I'm sure I can convince Alex to take us out to dinner for two of them, which eliminates at least a little bit of Margaret time. Jeez! And Lily had requested to take a few days off for Christmas. It didn't bother me when I thought it'd be only the four of us going to Aspen, but now that Margaret would be coming too, it's a whole different story. Not having a nanny isn't the end of the world, but it means that this vacation won't leave any time open for Alex and I to be alone. The thought gives me a pang of sadness, but maybe we could go back some other time by ourselves.

I towel dry and wrap my robe around myself, examining my reflection in the mirror. Alex and I both have a decent collection of winter clothing from living in Manhattan for so long, but I haven't skied in two years. I'll have to get some snow-proof clothes and shoes, a few different coats, and nice warm buntings for the twins. Picturing the kids playing on the snow with us brings a much-needed smile to my lips.

Winter is my favorite season and not even Margaret is going to ruin it! Come to think of it, I wonder if our trip is last-minute enough that the press won't get wind of it? The paparazzi were frantic during the lawsuits and even after we brought the babies home, but soon enough they discovered how boring we were in our normal day-to-day life. There were only so many photos that could be taken of Alex and me pushing a stroller. In Aspen, on the other hand, it would be fresh, new scenery with a host of different photo opportunities that would include his mom. If word gets out that we're headed there for Christmas, there might be trouble.

I shrug off my concerns and change into my leggings and crew neck sweatshirt for the evening. If they wanted to take pictures, so what? It'd just be more stroller-pushing... only in Aspen this time instead of New York.

Feeling a little more in control of my plans, I grab my laptop and notebook before jogging down the stairs to the dining room. The twins are already settled into their high chairs and are being spoon fed by Lily, who waves me off when I try to take over.

"Don't worry about it! Alex told me about your vacation plans... I'm willing to bet that you're itching to do some research." Lily's smile drops a little, and it seems she's unsure about her next question. "Are you... excited?"

I plop into one of the dining room chairs closest to the three of them after giving Jasper and Jasmine quick kisses on the forehead. "I'm resigned, and reluctantly optimistic."

"I understand," Lily responds with a nod. "Last minute plans and babies just don't mix, especially if they're vacation plans. But I'm sure you'll enjoy yourself."

I contemplate bringing up Margaret and getting Lily's thoughts on the whole ordeal, but that isn't fair to Lily. She's our live-in nurse and nanny, and always has a listening ear when I have questions about the kids, but burdening her with my inter-familial drama is probably crossing the line. I give her a tired smile, cracking open my laptop.

"Have you ever been to Colorado, Lily?" I ask.

She shakes her head. "If I wanted cold weather, I would just stay right here in New York." She appears to shiver a bit. "My family is originally from Jamaica, so the cold isn't my favorite thing in the world, as you can imagine. What will you guys be doing in Aspen?"

I shrug. "Well, skiing is what most people go for, and the mountain views of course. But there are some great hot springs, and all the Christmas events going on this time of the year. Lights, carolers, meeting Santa, horse-drawn carriages—oh! That's a great idea. Let me make a note of that."

I scribble down "carriages" on my list I had titled "*Distractions from Margaret*" while Lily wipes Jasmine's mouth, followed by Jasper's.

"It all sounds lovely," she comments as she cleans the twins' dinner up.

I make a noncommittal noise, scrolling through the attractions in the Aspen area with rapt concentration. I'm so involved that I jump when a mug of orange spice tea, steam coiling off it, is plonked down next to my laptop. I turn to see Alex, arms crossed, and an eyebrow raised.

"I made you some tea," he says blandly.

I scramble to shut my notebook, so he doesn't see my anti-Margaret plans. "Thanks, honey, all done with work stuff?" I ask, wrapping my hands around the mug he'd just given me.

"Yes." He glances at the empty high chairs. "I passed Lily on the way to the nursery. You, uh, want to watch a movie? Us and the kids?"

"A movie?" I repeat, reveling in his uneasiness. I smile at him, sipping my warm drink and remembering how cold, and then burning hot, he had made me earlier. "I'm not sure Jasmine and Jasper are at movie watching age."

"It's tradition, though," he insists. "*Frosty the Snowman* is on."

It's my turn to raise an eyebrow at him. "Seriously?"

Alex's face softens. "Let's just chill out, Petra."

It's such a silly idea and request that I can't help but be charmed by it. I nod, closing my laptop and Alex laces his fingers through mine as we walk to the living area for our Christmas movie evening.

The twins, already sleepy with their full bellies, are content to sit on our laps in the dark, all of us wrapped in warm fleece blankets as *Frosty the Snowman* plays on the screen in all its technicolor, claymation glory. I haven't seen the movie since I was a kid, but seeing Alex bounce Jasmine along to the songs, just to hear her little laugh, makes me realize he was right. Things like this can be Christmas traditions if we want them to be, and what better time to start than now?

Jasper has grabbed huge handfuls of my sweater and nuzzles his face into my middle, his eyelids heavy. I pull him close, and although he gives the movie more attention than I thought he would, it isn't long until his squirming has stopped and his breathing evens out. He's completely asleep.

I peek over at Alex and Jasmine to see the same scene. He gives me an indulgent smile. "I guess they had too big of a day to watch the whole thing."

At that moment, I yawn hugely, and Alex chuckles. "They aren't the only ones," I say.

"You want to put them to bed?" Alex suggests.

We should, but I don't really want to. Jasper's body is warm and heavy against me; he's already so much bigger than he was nearly six months ago, and I just want to take in this sweet little moment. Just a mom, a dad, and their two sleepy babies under the light of the Christmas tree.

"Let's wait awhile," I tell him in a whisper, and he nods.

I watch the children's movie, not really paying attention to it, just soaking in the peaceful night after such a tumultuous day. I think back on my anti-Margaret list, and all the activities I have already mapped out for us to do without her.

What does she have in mind? Is she looking for this little vacation as a way to get closer to me? If she thinks I'm gonna put my guard down, she's very mistaken.

I don't know if it's the movie playing, my thoughts surrounding Margaret, or my soft little Jasper sleeping in my lap, but my thoughts wander to my own mother. Did we ever have moments like this? Did she ever decorate a tree with me, or watch these silly movies? I honestly can't remember, but it all just makes me feel sad. My expression must reflect my thoughts, because Alex clears his throat softly.

"What are you thinking about?"

"Just… everything. I'm worried, Alex."

He can't move too much without jostling Jasmine, but he runs his sock-covered foot over my calf. "I know. Just trust me a little, alright? You can tell me anything, but just trust that I'm trying my best to do what I think is right."

I swallow hard, still feeling shaky, but I'll try to give him the benefit of the doubt and have faith. "Okay. I'm gonna do this...for you."

A few more quiet minutes pass before he asks, "Is there anything else, love? Any other reservations about this whole thing?"

I nibble my lip, wondering if what I'm about to say is shallow. "I know it seems stupid, but Emma and I worked hard picking out all these decorations and stuff. I hate to leave it all behind after the effort we put in."

Alex blinks a few times, looking pensive. It's clear he hasn't considered this. I can see the gears turning in his mind as he looks around our overly decorated living room. I giggle, seeing him wince at some of the gaudier decor.

"It will look nice, Petra. The villa should already be done up with proper Christmas decorations before we get there, and I made sure there is an enormous, natural tree too."

I sigh. I appreciate the effort, but I know what Alex's idea of a "proper Christmas" is. Whites, silvers, and golds. Reserved, expensive, and flawless. He just doesn't understand my drive and desire for a more colorful and childlike Christmas experience. But... at least he's trying.

I fake a grin for him. "Thank you. I'm sure it will be perfect."

We spend the rest of the evening talking softly about presents, what to buy the twins, and some of the Christmas traditions we both had as kids. The last subject leaves me feeling a little hollow, knowing that he and I both had

Christmases filled with expensive gifts but very little genuine affection and love.

Kissing my son's head, I vow it will be different from here on out. For all of us, not just Jasper and Jasmine. Alex and I will open presents on the floor with the kids, throwing wrapping paper everywhere and laughing. We'll make Christmas cookies and even leave some out for Santa. We will watch these goofy movies year after year, until we know every word. My babies will grow up with great Christmas memories.

We are going to have an amazing holiday in Aspen, Margaret and all her scheming be damned.

CHAPTER 2

Manhattan, December 22, 2021
Petra Van Gatt

"I'm really trying my best not to cry at your feet and beg you to come with us," I tell Lily, only half joking.

She laughs sweetly and hugs me. Her bags are loaded in the cab waiting downstairs, and I'm sure she is itching to get out of gray, slushy New York. Lily is spending the holiday with some of her extended family back in Jamaica, and she'll no doubt be unwinding from being my right-hand woman all these months.

"You're going to be perfectly fine," Lily insists.

I want to tell her I don't believe her, and that I'm nervous as heck about not having her be a text or intercom call away, but I also don't want her carrying any guilt into her vacation time. So I swallow my fears and plaster on a grin.

"I know you're right, but we're all going to miss you!" I assure her. Jasper and Jasmine, temporarily contained in the extra-large playpen we had set up in the living room, shout their agreement and rattle the sides of the pen. "See what I mean?"

Lily blows the twins a kiss before disappearing out the door, and suddenly, I'm alone. It's eight a.m. on December 22nd, and I'm completely running solo for the first time in months. Maria had taken off yesterday evening, after asking Alex at least a dozen times if there was someone to cook for us at the villa. He had laughed and assured the small woman that we would be well fed and taken care of, and she had finally left.

It's silly that I feel so strange being here by myself, but I just can't help it. I can't remember a time that Lily wasn't either helping me or was just a floor away in her basement apartment if I needed her. This really is a novel experience for me.

Alex texts me saying he's finishing a few things at work, and then he'll be home to take us to Teterboro for the flight. Dad and Catherine left this morning, so we might be the last ones to leave for Aspen.

After reading his SMS, I type, "I assume your mother is flying her broom down?" and briefly consider sending the message, but I decide at the last minute to delete it. Still, I give myself a good laugh.

After a much more polite query on my end, Alex informs me that Margaret is already on her way to our villa.

Our villa? I ponder the phrase, tapping my finger on my lips as I read the message over a few times. Surely Alex didn't mean that Margaret is staying with us? I want to grill him about it, but eventually I decide to let that slide too. Today is already going to be tense enough without Alex and I arguing. I'll find out the truth soon enough with my own two eyes, anyway.

I pocket my phone and sit on the floor next to the playpen, absentmindedly entertaining the twins while I wait on my husband. Today will be the twins' first time on a plane, and I'm already dreading the experience. Flying to Aspen takes between four and five hours, since we don't have any layovers, so it isn't an excruciatingly long flight, but still… Four to five hours with unhappy twin infants is never a good time; especially when you're not in the comfort of your own home. I wish it was as easy as a car ride, but the takeoff and pressure changes are sure to make their ears hurt, and with no way to bring them relief, they're going to be royally pissed for a while.

After we are safe in the air, I can take them out of their seats to console them, which should help a bit, but four hours is still a long time. I woke them up early today, at 5:30 a.m., hoping that they would be well and truly tired by take-off time and sleep through a good portion of the flight. If I could get them to sleep through takeoff, things would be even better.

"You two little muffins have no idea what's in store," I tell them.

Jasper has managed to crawl a few shaky paces, but Jasmine is still locomoting by rolling and scooting herself around. She doesn't get far, and she definitely isn't fast, but she is determined. Her pediatrician said that it's normal for her to be a bit behind with physical milestones, considering how small she is, but the fact that Jasmine seems so dead set on keeping up with Jasper is a good sign.

Sitting on my knees, I let them show me their toys one by one, babbling to each other and to me as they occupy themselves. Two sets of bright blue eyes watch me carefully examine each toy they hand me, excitedly snatching it back when I'm done.

"Fascinating," I say once I've finished giving a stuffed teal duck a thorough once over. "Here you go."

They squabble over the duck, Jasmine winning the tugging contest while Jasper sits in defeat, his bottom lip pushed out.

"Oh no, poor little prince. Come to mommy," I tell him, scooping him up and planting kisses all over his soft, chubby cheeks. I'm just about to switch out for Jasmine when the door opens and Alex enters, a beautiful smile stretching his lips upwards.

"Are we all ready to leave?" he asks, an excited tone in his voice. He clearly hasn't thought about how stressful the flight will be.

"Yup," I respond. "Help me get the seats and we'll get out of here!"

We snap the two wriggling babies into the car seats, tucking thick blankets around them for warmth once they are buckled safely. Alex seems to be in a rush, and I'm not sure why. It is his jet after all. It's not like it's going to leave without us.

I'm about to ask him what the deal is when he turns to me, Jasper's car seat held in one arm and our leather diaper bag slung across his chest. "Sorry, it's just that my Mom arrived way earlier than I anticipated."

I nod with a small smile, but wince once he turns back around. The last thing I needed to know is that Margaret has already arrived.

The drive to Teterboro is uneventful, besides Alex buzzing with excitement in the front seat beside the driver Zach. I'm sitting in the back between the car seats, determined to keep the twins awake so they would sleep through the flight. I tickle tiny feet and play over a dozen games of peek-a-boo, but I still feel like I'm losing the battle. Every time I turn to one twin to entertain them, the other's eyes get suspiciously droopy.

I'm sure I'm about to lose Jasmine to nap time when Zach blessedly pulls into the airport, sliding the car into the parking space effortlessly. The sky is spitting a disgusting mix of sleet and snow, and I wait patiently for Zach to get the huge umbrella out of the trunk so we can head inside.

The cold wakes the babies up fully, turning their little cheeks rosy. The inside of the small airport is wonderfully toasty, but it isn't long until Alex has confirmed all our details and we are headed out to the tarmac to board the jet.

I take one longing look over my shoulder at what little of the city I can still see before I climb the stairway into the plane. It's a familiar space, full of whites and creams, with huge seats up front and the small but fully functional living area in the back. I blow out an exhausted breath and strap Jasmine's car seat into the chair next to me before taking a seat myself.

Alex follows suit, and before I know it, we're ready for takeoff. I chew my bottom lip nervously, but Alex reaches across the aisle to me and lays a large, grounding hand on my knee. "We've flown so many times. It will all be okay."

I nod tightly, not completely convinced. The flight attendant checks on us briefly, but I decline the offer of any refreshments, my stomach roiling with anxiety. Motherhood has made me more perceptive of the dangers of everyday life, flying included, and I can't help the sinking feeling I'm experiencing as we prepare for takeoff.

Jasmine, on the other hand, has realized that she's finally been spared from my efforts of keeping her awake. I motion for Alex to pass me one of the prepared formula bottles out of the portable bottle warmer in the diaper bag, and I feed Jasmine a quick half-portion of milk.

"Not the entire bottle," I instruct Alex, who has followed my lead and is feeding Jasper. "We don't want them to get sick on takeoff."

"Right," he says, not looking up from feeding his son. There is a little wrinkle of concentration between Alex's brows, and it reminds me of the same one Jasper gets when he's thinking really hard about crawling or pulling himself up. It makes me giggle, and some of my tension flows away. Okay, we can do this. It's just a flight.

The twins, with their bellies full, doze off fully right before we take-off. I grip the arms of the seat, my knuckles white, but the babies sleep through the whole thing as we begin our ascent. I exhale slowly as everything evens out.

Take off completed, now we just have to make it through the flight itself and landing. I have no illusions that the kids will sleep the whole four hours, so my plan is to wake them up around hour three for the rest of their bottle, diaper changes, and whatever else they need at the time. The white noise of the plane engines and the low voices of the pilots and flight attendant talking help to sooth my nerves, and I settle back into my seat and let my muscles relax. Alex looks up from the laptop he had grabbed once Jasper fell asleep and gives me a patient look.

"So far, so good," he comments. "Why don't you go in the back and try to get some sleep? You look like you've been up all night."

I touch the thin skin under my eye, wondering how bad my dark circles are. Even though it's still early, it's been a busy morning, and a nap doesn't sound all that bad. I shoot a look at the sleeping babies before turning back to Alex, a questioning look on my face.

"Don't worry," he assures me. "If they wake up, I'll take care of them. Go on." He waves towards the back of the plane.

I relent, feeling relieved. Now that I'm acknowledging it, sleepiness is weighing my limbs down, and my jaw cracks as I yawn hugely. I don't even bother flicking the lights on in the plane's bedroom, I just crawl under the covers of the queen-sized bed. I leave the door open, and the daylight from the open door makes me feel a little better about leaving Alex alone with the twins. They're only a few steps away.

My nap is wonderfully deep and peaceful, at least for a while, but I'm awoken when I feel a weight sitting on the other side of the mattress. I open one eye to see Alex holding both twins in his arms. Jasper is on his way to crying, making unhappy noises while he rubs his eyes, while his sister pulls at her father's short hair.

"They're awake," he explains as I haul myself up into a sitting position against the headboard. "And a bit grumpy."

"I gathered that," I tell him, reaching my arms out. Alex hands me Jasmine, to the relief of his scalp, I'm sure. He plops Jasper down next to me on the bed before going back out front to grab their bottles.

"We're about an hour out." Alex tells me as he settles in next to the twins and I. "Think we can keep them entertained until then?"

"I don't think we have much of a choice," I say, stretching my arms over my head before taking one of the warmed bottles from Alex. Jasmine reaches out excitedly and I cradle her in my arms, letting her have her post-nap meal. "We're going to have to do a lot of that this week."

Alex hums in agreement, kicking his feet up on the bed and leaning over Jasper so he can feed him too. After a minute, he comments, "It will be fun."

I smile down at my daughter's little face, her sapphire eyes content as she drinks. "Yeah, it will."

CHAPTER 3

Aspen, December 22, 2021
Petra Van Gatt

The jet circles Aspen-Pitkin airport briefly, giving us enough time to drag ourselves and the twins out of the bed and get them back into their car seats. After their stint of freedom crawling and rolling around the bed while Alex and I tried to distract them with cartoons on the iPad, they are not thrilled to be going back into their confining car seats.

We'd avoided the ear-popping with the pressure change on takeoff, but we aren't so lucky during the descent. They have contented themselves to play with the baubles and mirrors hanging from the handle of their car seats at first, but it doesn't take long until they furrow their brows and start to pull at their earlobes.

It escalates to full-blown crying, which is only slightly alleviated by the pacifiers I give them halfway through. Once the plane touches down, I blow out a relieved breath, rubbing my temples to dissipate the headache building.

The pilot brings the plane to the stopping point, and we prepare to disembark, grabbing the diaper bag and discarded coats and blankets. It's amazing how chaotic a space can become in such a short time when six-month-olds are involved.

I'm trying not to be excited, to temper my expectations of this trip and accept that there is going to be a good dash of interpersonal drama with my dad, Catherine, and Margaret all present, but as soon as I get a glimpse out the plane window all my logic floats away like petals on the breeze. Oops. I'm excited.

Mountains loom over the town like guardians, massive and casting us in their shadows. The snow here is different from how it is in Manhattan. Instead of slushy and gray, everything is pristine and white, as if someone has delicately frosted all of Aspen in confectioners' sugar.

My heart warms up at the memories I have from here and especially my last trip here with Alex, two years ago. It's insane how fast time goes.

I'm internally kicking myself for leaving my mountain painting undone at home, because one look at the place has me itching to put a brush to canvas. It's like an artist's dream, inspiration wise. I hold Jasmine's carrier in the crook of one arm once we reach the bottom of the plane's stairs and use my free hand to dig my phone from my pocket and snap a few hasty pictures for later. Maybe there's an art store somewhere where I could pick up a travel kit.

"Roy and Catherine got in a few hours ago," Alex says, checking his own phone for messages. "They want to meet us at a cafe near their villa if you're okay with that?"

I slide my phone back into my pocket and nod. "Yeah, that's fine. I'm a little peckish, anyway."

We don't have a driver for our time in Aspen, but the Audi Q7 that Alex rented is waiting for us in the parking lot outside of the airport, car seat bases already installed. We click the chilly twins in, and Alex starts the vehicle up. I immediately turn on the heated seats, melting into the leather with a heavy sigh. *Alright, we're here. Let the Christmas wonder commence.*

The cafe is a good halfway point between the airport and the villa, and since it's a Wednesday, the traffic isn't too hectic. The closer we get to downtown, the more intense the Christmas decor around the city becomes; the kid in me wants to press my nose against the car window and take it all in. I can hardly wait for nighttime when everything is lit up.

Cafe Jour De Fete is nearly empty, the lunch rush having departed a few hours earlier, and it's easy for us to find the table near the back where Dad and Catherine are seated. Catherine's sporting dark snow pants and an elegant white turtleneck sweater but she doesn't bother standing as we approach.

Dad, thankfully, does rise, shaking Alex's hand before wrapping me in a quick embrace. He leans over to greet the twins, who both start to kick happily.

"Good to see you, kid," Dad says gruffly. "How was your flight?"

"It went as smooth as could be expected with the babies," I answer before turning to Catherine. "Good afternoon, Ms. Dubois," my voice is wary, unsure about the energy she's putting off.

"Oh please, call me Catherine," she says with a dismissive wave, offering me no greeting in return before she takes another sip on her cup of hot chocolate. Did the flight leave her in a bad mood? Alrighty then, I guess that's how things will be.

We've just sat down, Jasper held in my lap while my father holds Jasmine, when the bell of the entrance door tinkles, alerting us that someone else has entered the cafe.

If I was a little more dramatic, I'd say that the temperature in the place dropped significantly when Margaret walked in, but since my back was to the entrance, the only two things that clued me in were the tensing of my dad's shoulders and my husband rising up from his seat.

"Mother," I hear Alex say, his voice cautious, and I have to close my eyes to prepare myself.

I'd have liked to ignore Margaret the whole time, or pretend that she was invisible, but Alex's mother simply can't be ignored. Her presence seems to fill the small cafe, causing the room to shrink and the air to be thinner.

I look over my shoulder to see Alex and Margaret talking softly by the counter, Margaret wrapped in a white fur coat that seems to double her in size. Her pale silver hair is swept back into a classic bun on the back of her neck, and her ears are covered with white earmuffs that perfectly match her coat. She radiates wealth and importance, and I cannot help but roll my eyes at the whole thing.

I'm still watching Alex and his mom, but out of the corner of my eyes, I can see Catherine lean over to whisper something into my dad's ear. He shakes his head sharply, and Catherine sits back in her seat, mouth pinched. Uh-oh, I'm sensing some sort of conflict on the horizon. How will this all go down, I wonder.

Alex takes Margaret's coat when she shrugs it off, and she pulls down the earmuffs until they hang around her neck. She's dressed in a dark green turtleneck that looks incredibly soft to the touch, paired with dark tailored snow-pants and short-heeled booties. They clack on the tile floor as she comes over to us, eyes hungrily taking in first Jasper, who is in my lap, and then Jasmine, in my dad's.

Dad stands to greet her, and they exchange three-cheek kiss. Catherine, on the other hand, just smiles politely at her and I wonder silently if the two have ever met before. I know next to nothing about Catherine, but her presence may be enough of a distraction that Margaret's laser-focused attention won't be on me this whole time.

"Roy," Margaret says with a curt nod, her voice lightly accented and polished. "And my beautiful daughter-in-law, Petra. How are you, my dear?"

My spine tenses, but I try my best to keep it from showing on my face. "Fine," I bite out, my arms tightening around Jasper, who squeaks in response.

Margaret, seeming to have forgotten our last tense interaction, reaches out a perfectly manicured hand to stroke Jasper's cheek. Every instinct in me wants to slap her hand away, but Jasper, not being one for strangers, turns his head away on his own accord. Margaret pats his soft hair instead, looking slightly disappointed.

"They look wonderful, Alex. So healthy," she says, taking the teacup her son offers her as he returns. "May I hold one of my grandchildren?"

I stay silent, turning my body so she can't try to pluck my son from my embrace. Alex starts to say something, but my dad interrupts by holding Jasmine up slightly. "You can take her, Margaret," he says, before sliding me a look that reads "Don't argue."

I think about all the ways I'm going to scold my dad when we're alone for this breach of trust, but I shouldn't have worried. As soon as Margaret reaches down for Jasmine, she clutches my father's arms like a life raft, even going so far as to turn her head away from her paternal grandmother and lean heavily away.

Margaret looks more annoyed by the second. "Oh, will you just hand her here? She's just being contrary."

I've still only said one word to Margaret, because everyone keeps stealing my thunder when it's time to talk. This time, it's Catherine, who barks out a laugh loud enough that I jump.

"She obviously doesn't want you to hold her," Catherine says simply, sipping her drink, unbothered, when Margaret stares daggers in her direction.

"And you are?" Margaret inquires, voice dripping with icicles. She finally looks at Catherine fully, and I can't help but notice an odd moment pass between the two of them. It almost seems like the next few seconds are being read from a script.

"Catherine Dubois, but don't worry, I already know who you are, Ms. Van Dieren."

Margaret tilts her head slightly. "Has anyone ever told you that you look shockingly like Roy's ex-wife?"

Catherine fluffs her short, yellow-blond hair with one hand. "Yes, actually. Seems like Roy has a type. Say, Ms. Van Dieren, you knew Tess too, didn't you? Rather…personally?"

If the temperature had dropped when Margaret arrived, Catherine had just thrown us all into the Arctic Ocean. The silence is so deafening that it presses unpleasantly on my eardrums. Everyone is refusing to even breathe for a second, and my chest is tight with the shock of Catherine's words. Who exactly is this woman?

"*Catherine,*" Dad hisses, taking his girlfriend's arm in a tight grip. "I think it's time we head back to our villa."

Much to Jasmine's intense displeasure, my dad hands her over to Margaret, who takes her with a smug look on her face. Jasmine leans hard away from her grandmother, but

Margaret has her held quick. I shiver, seeing my daughter in her arms. It's one of the things I had hoped to never see in my lifetime.

"Yes," Catherine purrs. "Let's go back to our *private* villa. You're staying with your son, right, Ms. Van Dieren? I understand." Her smile turns wicked on her lovely face. "It's not every day you can see him."

The smug look is wiped from Margaret's face, and she visibly bristles at the veiled insult. Dad pulls Catherine towards the exit, but before they're out the door, something strange happens. Catherine digs her heels in before Dad can pull her out and turns back to us a last time.

"No hard feelings, Margaret?" she says, and it's such a pivot from her previous antagonistic attitude that it feels like whiplash. "Wouldn't want us to get off on the wrong foot."

Margaret is silent for a minute, gazing at Catherine neutrally until a smile pulls at the corner of her mouth. It almost seems like two worthy adversaries facing off, but with mutual respect being understood by both. Margaret nods curtly, and Catherine lets Dad pull her outside.

I look at Alex, who looks equally baffled. Did I miss something? He shrugs when I mouth, "*What in the heck was that?*"

"Roy always did like them feisty, so I've heard. More the pity, he needs a calmer influence at his age," Margaret comments as she sinks into the chair Catherine had abandoned. Jasmine gazes up at her dad with wet eyes, and Alex lets her grasp at his outstretched fingers, but doesn't remove her from his mother's arms like she truly wants.

"Now," Margaret continues. "Shall we discuss sleeping arrangements?"

Crap, I think miserably. *I guess we really are bunking together.*

***

"I thought you already understood that she was staying with us, Petra," Alex insists as we drive to the villa, tapping his fingers on the leather steering wheel.

"There's a difference between vacationing with us and staying in the exact same house," I grumble, sinking lower into the heated seat of the SUV.

"If it helps, the villa undertook a big extension last year," he offers, but I roll my eyes and watch out the window as we go, not wanting to look at him.

"The villa could be the size of a football field and it would still be too small to share with Margaret, but whatever. I don't want to talk about it anymore. She's already caused us to argue enough."

Alex exhales, but after a few moments, he slides a hand to rest on my knee. A peace offering. Resigned, I lay my hand over his. I meant what I said. I will not let Margaret's presence cause anymore strife between Alex and me. We've already bickered enough about it.

Margaret has taken a private driver to the villa, which is located on the top of a hill, a bit isolated from the rest of the city, but with the best views to downtown and the mountainous skyline.

After checking where my dad is staying, I realize the villa he booked is not too far from ours, and also includes an inner courtyard and pool, while the back seems to offer similar views. Good; at least if we need something they are only a short distance away.

Pulling up to the villa, a smile spreads up to my ears, recognizing the place we went to for my eighteenth birthday. Alex gives my hand a quick squeeze, as if he was reading my mind, before getting out of the vehicle.

It's so cold outside, but it doesn't faze me, bundled up in my new winter gear. I feel like a puffed-up marshmallow, but somehow Alex manages to pull his look off much better. He looks like a professional snowboarder, or maybe a distinguished ski instructor. The image makes me laugh, and it lightens my mood as we unload the kids and head inside.

The villa is exactly like I remember—all warm, welcoming neutrals, different colors of blunt wood, and gleaming chrome fixtures. Orange and red firelight reflects off enormous windows bracketing the living area, giving us an incomparable view of Colorado's natural beauty.

What I didn't expect was the thick, towering evergreen pine in the corner of the place, white lights twinkling, and piles of gifts wrapped perfectly and placed underneath. Attached to the stone fireplace mantle were four stockings, two silver and two gold. The rest of the villa is lovingly decorated too, the holiday accents looking like they had always been part of the townhouse. Nothing out of place, nothing awkwardly added.

Is it the rainbow Christmas I had wanted? No. Is it much more than I expected? Heck, yes. Out of the corner of my eye, I can see Alex watching my face, trying to gauge my reaction. His expression is carefully even, so I turn and offer him the most brilliant smile I can muster.

"It's gorgeous," I say, and he looks relieved, carefully setting Jasper's carrier down and cupping my face in his hands to kiss me softly.

"I'm glad you like it. It will do for now, won't it?"

"Of course it will," I purr, basking in his loving attention.

He kisses my mouth again, longer this time, before pulling away just enough to tell me, "You can thank me more thoroughly tonight."

I playfully slap his arm but let him link our fingers together afterwards and give me a quick tour of the refurbishment and extension the villa went through. The ground floor didn't change much, being the same sprawling and open concept with two suites, while the upstairs have been expanded to accommodate two more bedrooms, each one with an enormous bathroom—the smaller of the two having been prepared for the twins.

At the top of the stairs, the railing curls around, leaving an overhang where you can view the ground floor. It gives the place an airy, rustic vibe, even with all the state-of-the-art appliances.

"Let's go check our bedroom," Alex says as we go back downstairs and head to the place we share the best memories.

After we get inside, I notice our luggage has been delivered and is waiting for us by the door. A quick smile escapes me—this time the porter didn't leave mine in the other guest bedroom. Then my eyes alight on the beautiful scenery presented on the other side of the floor-to-ceiling windows in front of me. It has been two years, but the view is just as breathtaking as before. Afterwards my attention goes to the bed which is enormous, and looks to be made almost completely of whole logs fitted together, with red plaid sheets and an enormous white comforter topped with a quilt made of even more plaid.

I sink into the bed when I try to take a seat, and it's everything I can do to not snuggle into it and zone out for a little while. Sure, the plane nap had been great, but there is something to be said about a pillowy mattress, fluffy blanket, and snow falling outside the crystal-clear windows. It's perfectly cozy.

Alex leaves me there, heading out to greet the butler who has just arrived with a cheery "Hallo!" from the foyer. I kick off my fuzzy boots and let myself go boneless before my husband reappears in the doorway.

"No more sleeping," Alex warns from the doorway, depositing the Pack 'n Play on the floor. "You can sleep back in Manhattan."

I shake my head. "Just put the kids in their cribs and come lay here with me for a while," I suggest, patting the mattress beside me. Alex scoffs and ignores me, assembling the Pack 'n Play.

"The butler's name is Earl," Alex explains as he works. "I left the twins in their seats with him while I set this up. He looks to be about three-hundred years old, but I'm sure he's great. I guess we have a cook, too, George, and yes, before you ask, I warned them you're vegan."

"Thanks, babe," I murmur, only half paying attention.

"You *should* thank me," Alex quips. "If I have to turn away any more complementary charcuterie trays, I may lose my mind."

"Hilarious."

"Come on," he says once he's finished setting the play pen up. Alex grabs me by my limp wrists and hauls me, unwillingly, into a sitting position. I'm dead weight, but he's persistent, and it isn't long until I've tugged him down with me, and we're both laughing, facing each other with our noses almost touching, legs tangled together.

"My lazy wife," Alex complains, touching our foreheads together.

"Hey now. You have no idea the things I have planned. This vacation is going to knock your socks off. You'll see."

Alex hums. "As long as there is time for the special trip I've set aside."

That piques my interest. I raise up on an elbow, looking down at him and the mischievous glint in his eye. "What is it?"

Alex puts a finger on my lips. "Hush. It's a surprise."

I bat his hand away. "Give me a hint, at least."

He rolls to his back and folds his hands behind his head. "Okay, one hint. Bring a swimsuit." He seems to consider something for a moment before wrinkling his nose and adding, "*Not* the one from the swim class, though."

"Asshole," I gasp in mock offense. "That's my favorite suit and you know it!"

"Get your eyes checked when we get home, then."

I poke him in the side, which leads to us wrestling around the bed again until somehow Alex is on top of me with my hands pinned above my head. In the span of a second, I'm aware of his denim-clad thigh pushed between my legs and the rasp of his stubble on my cheek as he leans over to whisper in my ear.

"Got you," he says, voice rough. "Now what am I going to do with you, my overly tired wife, with horrible fashion sense?"

I turn my head to meet his lips, a shiver skittering across my skin, but before I can truly kiss him, we both hear the entrance door creak open, followed by Margaret's voice calling, "Alex! Hello!"

Alex groans, letting go of my hands and rolling off me. I whimper a complaint, but he ignores my protest, straightening his shirt and collar in the mirror before making his way to the door. He pauses right before leaving the room and glances at me over his shoulder.

"Go ahead and start unpacking, I'll deal with Mom and the kids."

"Maybe we should get one of the rooms upstairs to be closer to the twins?" I ask. Despite loving this bedroom due to the view, I'm pretty sure the view from the ones upstairs must be just as good.

"We'll see," he answers, before closing the door behind him to give me some privacy. Knowing him like I do, that means more like a no than anything else.

I'm not tired anymore. Alex has me worked up, and if I didn't know any better, I might think that was his plan all along. Blowing out a breath, I unzip my suitcase and sort my things out in piles: needs to be hung up, casual clothes, pajamas, undergarments. The piles are rather large… but I like to be prepared. One never knows what life can throw at you.

I shoot a text out to Emma, letting her know that we've arrived safely.

Freezing your tits off yet? Emma messages back, and I snort.

As of right now, my tits are safely inside the villa AND my sweater, thank you very much. They're quite toasty, I respond.

She must have been scrolling Twitter, because she texts back again right away. *Yeah, for now. In other news, I've got a little bit of info for you on Catherine, but I want to do a little more digging b4 I give my full report, ok?*

For sure. Thanks again, I reply back.

Hm. It's definitely interesting that she's found some good gossip about Catherine already. That at least lets me know that there is more than meets the eye. She's not just a middle-aged widow looking for love, I guess. For a second, I feel a pang of guilt snooping on my dad's girlfriend. He might be a workaholic, and he has strained our relationship for most of our lives, but I still want him to be happy. Hopefully, whatever Emma digs up isn't so bad that I have to blow the entire relationship out of the water.

Once I'm done throwing my things in their appropriate storage area, I grab the duffle bag full of the twins' things, planning to put them away in the makeshift nursery. I'm sure Earl wouldn't mind unpacking for us all, but every time a housekeeper or butler does it for me, I'm completely confused on where everything ends up. As a serial late-arriver, sometimes I just need to grab and go.

I'm enjoying the feel of the plush carpet under my bare feet when I hear Margaret's voice drift up from the living room, clear as a bell here in the other side of the hallway. As I look towards the door, I notice Alex hadn't closed it completely, he had just pushed it against the doorframe, leaving a small gap.

"Oh please, Alex. She clearly can't stand the sight of me." Margaret huffs.

I open the door and dare a few steps towards the hallway until I can just see her and Alex's heads standing in front of the fireplace, Margaret waving one hand dismissively while the other arm holds a supremely displeased Jasmine against her body.

I bristle. Of course, she took the first opportunity she could to get her scaly hands on my children. I try to push down the sound of blood rushing in my head so I can hear them talk more clearly.

"Maybe if you acted warmly for once in your life, she wouldn't feel that way," Alex responds. Jasper is sitting happily in his embrace, watching the situation play out with his classic wide-eyed gaze.

I can see Margaret pinch her lips together, probably holding back some smarmy remark, but she thinks better of it and exhales, shoulders sagging. "I will try, Alex. I will, if it means the chance of having my family back in my life. Part of it at least."

It's a sweet speech, but I can see how torn it makes Alex from the strained expression on his face. I, for one, don't believe a word of it. Alex massages the bridge of his nose with his free hand. "Mother…"

Margaret waves her hand in the air again, as if blowing the rest of his words away. "Let's not discuss it right now. We're all a bit tired and need to settle in." Her gaze slides to the fire, as if she can't look at Alex as she asks the next question. "Could I… embrace you, son? I have missed you, whether or not you believe it."

Don't do it. I think desperately, but of course Alex can't hear my internal pleas. His shoulders stiff and body vibrating with uncertainty, Alex steps close to his mother and gives her a one-armed hug, barely an embrace at all because of the babies they both hold. I can't see Margaret's face over Alex's tall form, but when they pull away, I think I see a small shiver pass through her.

I feel nauseous, my stomach in knots. I press a fist to my offending abdomen and back slowly away, silently grabbing the twins' luggage again and fleeing upstairs towards the nursery, away from the strangely private scene between mother and son that I feel incredibly uncomfortable observing.

***

A few hours pass while I unpack for the twins, but the fluttery, nervous feeling in my stomach refuses to abate. I push it aside, eventually going downstairs to get the twins so they can go for their afternoon nap. They've done a lot of sleeping today already, but even if they don't completely go to sleep, having them safely in their cribs will give me time to shower and get ready for dinner.

I had planned on cajoling Alex into taking us out tonight so I could avoid his mother, but he beat me to the punch by informing me that the cook had already been preparing dinner for us this evening. Resigned, I decide to flee back to the sanctuary of our rooms and have a nice long soak in the jacuzzi tub before dressing for the meal.

With the twins placed in their pale wooden cribs, complete with soft blankets and the ever-present heart rate monitors tucked under the sheets, I turn on some soft music for them and return to my room. After a plane ride and unpacking all our belongings, I'm dying to wash off and refresh.

The bathroom attached to the master suite is covered in white and gray tiles, with an open rainfall shower-head, and a sinfully large jacuzzi. I'm almost giddy as I draw the bath, adding some of the rosemary and lilac oils that were provided.

Sinking into the steaming water is heavenly. It takes away any remaining chill from outside, and I can feel my muscles unwinding slowly.

Finally alone, I let myself consider the upcoming days. We have reservations at the Silver Queen Gondola tomorrow morning, and I'm hoping afterwards Alex and I can do some last minute Christmas shopping at all the adorable boutiques downtown. The gondola trip is supposed to be a surprise, and I hope it doesn't all unravel at the last minute like so many of our plans seem to.

I'm still not completely sure what our plans for Christmas Day are, if I'm being honest. In the hustle of preparing for this last-minute vacation, I had lost sight of how little time there actually was before the big day.

I sink down into the jacuzzi, considering. At least I had been able to get the delivery address for the special gift I had commissioned for Alex changed to the villa and not to the condo. I had hired a designer in Manhattan to make Alex a wool peacoat, but instead of polished wood buttons, the buttons are made from mother-of-pearls sourced from the island where we had our honeymoon. I hope it will be a nice call back to simpler times in our lives, and whenever he looks at the buttons, he'll be reminded of those blissful days spent under the blazing Seychellois sun.

I've dunked my head beneath the water when a muffled knock sounds at the bathroom door.

"Can I come in?" Alex asks.

I give him the affirmative, and he opens the door just wide enough to slide in before closing it again behind him, saving as much of the precious heat in the bathroom as he can. He raises his eyebrows, giving my body, concealed beneath the scented water, a thorough once over.

"Join me," I offer, folding my arms on the rim of the tub. "There's plenty of room."

Alex hesitates before turning the lock on the door handle and undressing. He's beyond handsome as he shirks the layers upon layers of winter clothes to reveal his lithe body and the muscles shifting underneath his skin. He looks perfectly bronzed and tan, almost like he should be in some paradise somewhere and not in this snowy town. I smile indulgently, making room for him as he lowers his powerful form down next to me.

He hisses, recoiling from the water before slowly lowering himself down again. "This water is hotter than hell."

"Don't be so dramatic," I tell him, flicking water at him from the tips of my fingers.

He grumbles but settles in on the other side of the tub. It's so huge that only our ankles intertwine. We're silent for a minute, both of us soaking up the warmth in the heavy air and the peacefulness of just being together. It's both intimate and comforting.

Alex's eyes are almost glowing, brilliantly blue and lit from within. He curls a finger at me, inviting me over into his space, and after a little bit of adjusting, I'm cradled against his chest, my back to his front, and his arms locked possessively around me.

"Even if you've fought me every step of the way," he says against my wet hair. "I'm glad to be here with you, wife."

"Hmm," I reply, drawing circles in the water with my fingers. "I think I'm glad, too. I'll let you know for sure later."

"Ungrateful girl," he quips, squeezing me a bit tighter until I squeak.

I try to poke him in the ribs, but he holds me fast. After a few seconds of struggling, I relent, going limp again in his grasp and letting myself be held in his embrace. I hate to ruin the moment, but in the quiet of us just relaxing together, I still feel that upset feeling in my gut.

"Alex," I begin. "I heard you talking to your mom earlier."

He sighs. "She's been so cold and strange. I mean, she wanted to do Christmas in the Netherlands, but I insisted if she wanted to do it with us, she had to be the one to come over."

What? I wasn't even aware that Margaret had insisted for us to go with the kids to the Netherlands. What's her problem? That woman is beyond ungrateful!

"Now she seems to be almost happy to be here, in her own weird way."

I think about my own mother, and bite my tongue, choosing my words carefully. "Why exactly won't anyone else in your family spend the holidays with her? Paris or Germany isn't that far."

He makes a speculative noise, and his chest vibrates against my back. "I don't know, maybe for the same reasons you don't want her here, I suppose. Well, sort of..." he trails off, and the ghost of Tess Hagen seems to hang in the surrounding air.

"I know what you mean," I say quietly.

"All my sisters told her they had plans, but they probably just didn't want to bother with her scheming."

"Or maybe that was just a plan your mom set up with your sisters to look like you had no other option left but to invite her over," I tell him tensely, but I try to move us away from that line of thought. Too little, too late. "Oh well... she's here now."

"Mmhmm," Alex hums.

A thought pulls at my mind, and I almost smirk. "I guess we know where Yara gets her lovely personality and social skills from."

"Oh God, Petra. Can we stop talking about my family while we're naked in the bath?"

"I'm just trying to keep up, you know. I feel like if I'm going toe to toe with them, I need to understand them. And maybe even be a little more like them."

Alex runs a hand down my shoulder, putting his lips on the nape of my neck, telling me softly, "Please don't do that. What I love about you is that you *aren't* like them, or like any of the other women I've known. You grew up around all of this nonsense, but it never permeated your spirit. You're still pure and good. I don't want you to become conniving."

I soften, turning my face so our lips touch in a whisper of a kiss. "Are you sure? I hate thinking that you're going to be stuck with a silly wife who is blind to everything going on around her."

"For one," he starts, "you're never blind. You're incredibly perceptive, even if you don't let on that you are. And two, your open, loving heart keeps me grounded, Petra. Never change."

I drag my lips over his again before rotating in his arms until I'm straddling his waist. Alex makes a strangled noise in his throat, grabbing my thighs, his fingers denting my soft flesh.

"Fine," I tell him. "But only if you show me right now how much you love me, just as I am."

Over the next hour in the bath, he doesn't answer me with words, but somehow I still get the message.

***

Feeling utterly relaxed and satisfied, I finish braiding my slightly damp hair back and start on my makeup. I want to look natural, but still put together enough that I won't draw any condescending looks from our unwanted dinner guest. I dip my makeup brush in a taupe shadow and start working it into the crease of my eye when my phone rings.

Emma's lovely face flashes across my screen. I hop up and shut the door of the bedroom, wanting some privacy for this conversation. Emma is sure to have some news for me, if our last text talk a few hours ago means anything, and I have a few tidbits to tell her, too. I'm sure she will not like what I have to say.

I pop my AirPods into my ears and answer the call, wanting to be hands free so I can finish my face. "Hello, Ms. Hasenfratz," I say when I answer.

"I hope I'm not interrupting your Hallmark movie moment in Aspen," Emma replies, her cheeky tone already on.

Thinking back to the last hour with Alex, I feel my cheek heating. "Maybe a little R rated for Hallmark, if I'm being honest."

"Gross," Emma comments. "Let's not get into details."

"Fine by me," I say with a laugh. "So what's up?"

"My peeps have done some serious digging into this Catherine Dubois, and some stuff doesn't quite add up," she tells me, her joking tone becoming more serious.

"Wait," I cut her off before she could get into it. "Did I tell you she came here with my dad to spend Christmas with us?"

"Really?" Emma snaps.

"And not only her," I add, keeping the best part for the end. "Someone else also came to join us all the way from the Netherlands…"

"Who?" she asks instantly.

I lower my voice, making sure I won't be heard from the outside and say, "The one and only Margaret Van Dieren."

"No shit!" Emma shouts. "She's there?"

"Yep, and staying at the very same villa as us," I add, nearly whispering.

"If this isn't some weird coincidence…" Emma points out, her words trailing off. "That might explain a few things."

"Like what?"

"Well," Emma says happily as she moves on to other subjects. "I think it's time for me to fill you in. Because weirdly enough, we're going to dive into even more of your husband's family. How do the Van Dierens seem to have a hand in every piece of drama?"

I scrunch one eye closed, curling my lashes in a failed attempt to finish my makeup. "What do you mean? Catherine is tangled up with the Van Dierens?"

"Sort of," she says. "See, Catherine used to be married to a man named Paul Dubois, who was independently wealthy. I couldn't find much about Catherine before her marriage, but I can confirm she comes from a French noble family…

who declared financial bankruptcy six months before she tied the knot." Holy shit! My mouth gapes open at the news. "Anyway, Paul was known to be a philanthropist and introduced her to one of his very dear friends: Sebastian Van Den Bosch."

"No," I breathe, shocked. "As in Julia and Sebastian Van Den Bosch?"

"Exactly," Emma confirms. "Catherine and Julia became close, even closer than Paul and Sebastian. They seemed to fund some of the same charities, and were almost inseparable for a time, my team found plenty of pictures of them together at philanthropic dinners—the Van Den Bosches and Duboises were always sitting at the same table. They even used to go on vacations together." Damn, my heart skips a few beats at the revelation. "Ten years ago, Paul and Catherine divorced—a very nasty divorce by the way—and she disappeared from the public eye for some time. There isn't much about Paul, either, but then Catherine shows back up recently with your dad at a few receptions here and there but with a total makeover—blonde, short hair, nose reduction, skinnier..."

"Jeez," I mumble as I mull it over in my head. I remain silent for a moment, tapping my makeup brush against my pursed lips. All of Emma's information is buzzing in my brain, but I haven't quite figured out how it all pieces together yet. If Catherine and Julia were close friends and attending the same events, that should mean Margaret would at the very least have known about her in passing, right? An alarm starts to sound deep in my psyche.

"Emma," I start, working out my thoughts as I speak. "Dad introduced Margaret to Catherine when we all arrived, as if they were strangers. And then, out of the blue, the women started to argue. That's weird, right? Margaret would have to know Catherine."

Emma hums on the other side, lost in thought too. "I mean, if she is using the same name she used when she was married, then yeah, I would think they'd have to know each other."

An idea suddenly occurs to me, and it chills me to the bone. I pull out an AirPod, listening to make sure there is no one hovering outside the door. I hate the thought I'm having, but the more I think about it, the more the pieces fit together. Catherine used to be very close to Julia and Sebastian Van Den Bosch. Now that she's divorced, she has been with my dad and they were introduced at a business event by "*friends in common.*" What if it were the Van Den Bosches who did the introduction? Maybe in the precise intent to play the matchmakers? But why my dad though? I mean, with the amount of men out there, why him in particular? As I keep pondering, the Van Den Bosches know that Dad and I have reconciled, and especially after the death of my mom, we have been much closer than before, so any leverage Catherine can have over my dad…

"Can be used against me," I say in disbelief, all the blood draining from my face.

"What?" Emma asks, confused.

I shake myself, my heart racing. I explain everything to Emma, and while at first she seems dubious, by the end of me explaining my theory, she sees the sense in it. "After Margaret and Catherine argued, they had this weird moment of making up with each other. If they continue to get along… then I think I'm right. I think Catherine is a plant set up by Margaret and Julia," I finish, having laid out everything on the table.

Emma whistles a low note. "This is some soap opera shit, Petra. Like, why would they want to use your dad like that to have leverage over you? That doesn't make any sense. Every dirty secret you know about them involves your husband, so it's obvious you're not a threat."

"Well…" I purse my lips together, not knowing how I can tell her what I have in mind without creating some serious damage between us. "Not all dirty secrets I know involve my husband, no. And Margaret knows that."

"What do you mean?"

"Um…" I'm left speechless as I search for the best way to start. "Are you and Yara still together?"

Emma is silent on the other side of the line, probably taken aback by my sudden question.

"Why do you want to know that?" she asks, her tone coming off more aggressive than usual.

After all, we had mutually promised not to talk about her relationship with Yara, but with Margaret being under the same roof as me for the next few days, I feel like Emma should know that Margaret is aware of the affair. I want Emma to be happy, even if that means continuing her fling, but this might be the reason why they have sent Catherine to be a plant.

It'd be a social catastrophe if I told even a single person about Yara and Emma, and Margaret knows it. Being one of the few people that knows of the affair means I hold a tremendous power over Margaret, and the only real danger is that she will try to make Emma's life harder. I have to make sure Margaret stays on the straight and narrow regarding my friend's relationship.

Not that I care what happens to Yara, but unfortunately, whatever happens to her affects Emma, too.

"You don't have to answer," I assure Emma. "I just needed to know because, um..." Words are hard to come by when you have to admit something like this to your best friend. "I might have told Margaret about you and Yara."

"What the fuck!" Emma shouts in astonishment. "Why the hell did you do that?"

Guilt hits me hard like a truck and I close my eyes at the blow. Yet, despite hating this moment more than anything, I owe her an explanation. "It was at the Cathedral when she came for the twins' baptism," I disclose for the very first time. "I wanted her to stay away from us once and for all, so I decided to use that secret to have leverage."

"Fuck," Emma mutters, letting out a loud breath in annoyance. "I can't believe it. Damn it! You're my best friend for fuck's sake!" she rebukes non-stop, and there's not much I can do if not agreeing with her. "Why did you have to use *my* secret for her to leave you alone?"

I shut my eyes tight, feeling just as disappointed with myself. "I know," I mumble feebly. "I'm so sorry, Emma, I shouldn't have done that, but she killed my mom," I remind her, my voice nearly quivering at the end. "The last thing I wanted was to see her ever again."

Emma doesn't answer right away, and it seems like the comment about my mom has eased the tension a bit. "I'm so lost right now..."

"Please, don't be mad at me, I never thought she'd come here to Aspen after what I told her. I'm so sorry. I've been fighting to have her not come with us since I found out. I hoped that she wouldn't come honestly, and that she was just saying she would as a way to make me freak out."

"Fuck," is all Emma says.

"I'm not going to bring you and Yara up once, I promise. And maybe she doesn't want to think about it, either, knowing it would ruin her family if word got out."

Emma takes a few deep breaths, considering me. "Well, you might be the only person on Earth with leverage over Margaret right now, so I don't think it's a coincidence that she's there." I can hear the clicking of Emma's fingers on her laptop's keyboard over the phone, and I wonder if she's typing a frantic email to her lover. "You know I don't care what the public thinks of me," Emma continues, "but Yara does. Her marriage with Elliot..." Emma spits the word *marriage* like it's poison. "It means something to her. I'm not sure *what*, but something." Given the fact Yara has his name branded on her skin, I can only assume the same.

"It will be okay," I try to reassure my friend, feeling heartbroken for her. "I think she is here just to make my life a living hell. She's only here for a few days. That's not long enough to manipulate me into anything. I think this is all about ruining the holidays for me. I don't think you're going to get pulled into anything."

Emma leaves me with another bout of silence, and what she says next cracks my heart even farther. "I hate knowing you and my godchildren are there with that psycho. Margaret holding my little princess..." Shockingly, I think I hear a hitch in Emma's voice. Emma, one of the strongest people I know, never cries. I hear a small sniffle and a muted "fuck" before she comes back to speak, her normal aloof voice in place. "Petra, I don't think you should be alone. Alex is great and all, but I don't know if he can be unbiased around her. I'm going to come up to Aspen to be with you."

I blink a few times, taken aback. How did we go from sharing information about my dad's girlfriend to Emma offering to come be my backup? Absolutely not. She doesn't need to be here, facing Margaret, who I know Emma is a little frightened of, only because she could ruin her relationship with Yara. I shake my head, even though Emma can't see me.

"No, Emma, I've got this. It's really only a few days. Trust me, okay? She won't do anything to us, don't worry."

Emma exhales in relief and sounds much more like her normal self. "Yeah, okay, if you're sure. But please, be careful with Margaret, alright? God knows what she's capable of."

"I will," I say warmly.

"And you need to watch your step," she adds, concern thick in her tone. "If what you said about Catherine is true, you'll have to warn your dad."

"I know," I say shakily.

"Poor Roy," Emma comments. "Being used like that is really fucked up. Especially if he really likes her."

Ugh, I hadn't even thought that far yet. If Catherine *is* a plant, then Dad is going to get his heart broken. With a knot in my throat, I say, "Yeah. Poor Dad."

We're both quiet for a minute, the enormity of these claims laid out before us. If all of this is for real, then I've got a lot more on my hands than an awkward vacation. But either way I'll have to play it cool if I want to find out the truth.

"Emma, I love you. Have I told you that lately?" I comment after a bit, wanting to lighten the mood before getting off the phone with her. Suddenly, all of this drama could very well include her, too.

"Get in line," Emma tells me with a chuckle. "Call me in the morning, okay? Or at least sometime tomorrow. I want to know everything."

"I absolutely will. If we're right, you're the only one I'll be able to talk to about this. I can't tell Alex until I'm completely certain."

"Agreed. Be careful out there, snow princess."

"I will. Bye."

I remove my AirPods gingerly, setting them on the vanity and resting my freshly powdered face in my hands, gazing absentmindedly at my reflection. Despite the heavy news from Emma, I had pulled my makeup off well enough, and my face glows with health, my tight braid making me look fierce and no-nonsense.

Standing to grab my clothes off the bed, I straighten my spine and make myself a promise. If Margaret wants a fight, she'll get one. And I'm not going to lose.

***

The right clothes can be like a suit of armor. They can change your entire outlook on life and give you confidence you never expected to have. I had felt that way, confident and armored, in a perfectly tailored violet silk cold shoulder shirt, black booties, and blue-black designer jeans, when I had crossed the hallway an hour ago to have dinner with my harpy mother-in-law.

Except, of course, I'm the mother of twins—her grandchildren. Which is why I'm scraping butternut squash puree off of my gorgeous shirt in the bathroom while dinner continues for everyone else. *This is just my luck.*

It had started out as a lovely dinner, all things considered. The table was long and grand, the antiqued wood shined until it sparkled. There was no tablecloth, just linens at each table setting in shades of reds and golds. In the center of the rustic table, there was an old glass milk jug, up-cycled into a charming vase and filled to bursting with fresh flowers, despite the time of the year.

Flames were burning in the fireplace which were taller than I am, and the radiant heat was like a warm hug the moment you entered the dining room.

Alex had given me a knowing grin, no doubt recalling our recent tryst in the bathtub, and our children were dressed in comfortable one-piece outfits, warm and apparently starving if their huffs and squeals were anything to go by. It was a perfect family portrait that I was happy to join.

Except, of course, seated on one side of my husband was his mother, looking for all the world like a queen reigning over her kingdom, her sharp chin held high. She gave me a polite nod, but I know I saw a glint of hostility in the depths of her gaze. I didn't return even that small greeting, instead choosing to sit next to Alex, giving him a quick peck on the cheek before doing the same to Jasmine and Jasper.

"Ma ma ma ma MA," Jasmine insisted, reaching to be let out of her high chair prison. I shook my head and booped her on her button nose.

"Not yet, little princess. We have to eat first."

Jasmine screamed her protest, causing her brother to stick out his lower lip in a pout of disappointment.

"Is the cook warming up the baby food Lily sent with us?" I asked Alex, and he had shaken his head.

"George says that anything eaten under this roof will come from his kitchen and his kitchen alone," Alex said with a laugh. "He was adamant."

"Whatever." I shrugged, reaching for my glass of iced cucumber lemon water and taking a sip. "I just hope he hurries before the twins revolt."

"It seems to me only little Jasmine is protesting," Margaret intones, but I ignore her.

I pushed the paper straw down into my glass, covering the top hole with a finger to trap some water inside before offering it to Jasmine. She opened her mouth, displaying empty gums, and greedily drank the refreshing offering. I offered Jasper the same, and he drank too, but screwed up his face at the taste.

"I guess cucumber isn't his thing," I chuckled.

Before I could give them a second taste, one of the strangest looking men I'd ever seen emerged from the kitchen, carrying a few plates while another man followed with more.

The cook was wearing checkered chef pants and a white coat, as if he was working in a Michelin star restaurant and not a villa in Aspen. He was tall, around Margaret's age, but his posture was slightly stooped and a round paunch of a belly pressed against the lower buttons of his coat.

He had wispy, dark hair that came to a point in the front, and an equally sparse beard. The entire picture was finished by his scowling expression, the lines of his forehead pressed together in obvious wrinkles. He looked very odd, but at the same time, so freaking familiar!

I wracked my brain as the man distributed the meals, glistening butternut squash raviolis in a cream sauce with wilted spinach, and it wasn't until he set my plate down with a sullen, "I hope you enjoy, madame," that I realized who he reminded me of.

Holy crap, I had thought. *He looks exactly like the Grinch!*

My laughter had bubbled over until I couldn't help but guffaw, but quickly coughed into my hand to disguise the noise. Alex looked at me, concerned, and I waved him off, planning on explaining later.

Chef George returned to the kitchen to bring out dinner for the children, and my eyebrows shot up to my hairline with surprise.

"For the small masters of the house, I have prepared a butternut squash puree with browned butter and mint garnish," he said, presenting the small bowls to my baffled-looking children, before placing them down on the high chairs with a flourish and departing.

"It looks delicious," Margaret commented.

Forgetting for a moment that I was ignoring her, I answered, "It does, wow."

The ravioli was probably incredible, but I didn't get to try any yet since the twins had immediately wanted to sink their little fists into their gourmet dinner. So while Alex and Margaret made stilted small talk, I started feeding the babies.

The butternut puree smelled divine, at least, and eventually I'd be able to try out that ravioli. Jasmine and Jasper also approved, so much so that it was almost impossible to keep up with them both. As soon as I scooped a bite into one waiting mouth, the other baby was fussing for their next spoonful. I was keeping up valiantly for a few minutes, but I had made a critical error by leaving the bowls on the trays of their high chairs. As I reached over to feed Jasper, Jasmine decided she was done waiting, hitting the corner of the bowl with a quick slap, just hard enough that it fell from the tray…

And all over my chest.

Conversation between the two other adults at the table had ceased, and I could see Earl puttering over to help. Suddenly, being the food-covered center of attention was humiliating, and I stood up, the bowl falling to the floor with a clatter. Jasmine watched it all happen in silence, her sweet face devoid of any pity for her mother, simply wondering when her next bite was coming.

My face had flushed bright red. "I…uh, I'm going to go clean up. Be right back," I stuttered.

Alex stood. "Do you need help?"

"No. Nope. I'm good," I said in a rush, power walking to the bedroom and completely avoiding looking at Margaret, afraid to see a smug look on her face. The hallway had seemed to be the longest of my entire life, but I had finally made it to our bathroom, where I was right now.

"Dammit," I sigh, stripping off my shirt before I rinse it in the sink and then throw it into the laundry basket in the bathroom's corner. It's a lost cause, for tonight anyway.

Resigned to my fate, I bypass my drawers and pull open Alex's, grabbing a gray crewneck sweatshirt of his that has a small BRIONI emblazoned across the front in darker gray lettering. It's huge on me, but I push up the sleeves and give myself a quick once over in the mirror. I guess if I can't rub it in Margaret's face that I'm young and beautiful, I'll show her that her son belongs to me, so much so that I can wear his clothes.

Not only that, but his sweatshirt, worn and soft from dozens of washings, is crazy comfortable. It's a win-win.

I head back down the stairs briskly, sliding my hand down the railing as I go. I don't want the twins to wait too long to finish their meal, plus I'd like to get them fed before my food gets too cold for me to enjoy.

When I reach the bottom floor, I pause. Margaret has moved to my seat, and is feeding both kids, a spoon in each hand. She looks comfortable, like this isn't the first time she's had to feed two little ones at once. I come up short, stopping in my tracks, and give Alex an uncomfortable look. He knows how I feel about Margaret messing with the kids.

Alex shrugs, and motions for me to sit next to him in the chair Margaret previously occupied. Margaret must see Alex move, because she glances over at me. "Oh, Petra, go ahead and eat, dear. I'm already finished, I can handle these two."

I want to argue, but the look on Alex's face says, *Please don't make this difficult.* My shoulders sag in defeat, and I give up easier than I would have liked. It must be because of how hungry I am.

Someone, either Alex or Margaret, has moved my plate and drink over to her previous seat. I sit down, watching Margaret warily. Jasper is clearly just happy to be fed, but Jasmine is still cautious of this new person. Not cautious enough to refuse the food she's being offered, mind you, but she isn't quite as comfortable as her brother. Assured that they are eating, I relent and start on my own meal.

It's rich, the flavor coating my tongue, and I savor each bite of pasta and spinach. Alex looks at me, pleased to see that I'm eating. "Do you approve, lady of the house?"

I nod, my mouth full, before swallowing. "It's delicious. Seriously."

His plate is already empty, and he's slowly working on a glass of dark, amber colored whisky which he swirls in his glass. "I'm glad to stay in tonight, but I'll also be glad to do some exploring tomorrow. Did you say you had something planned for us, Petra?"

"Yes!" I say between bites. "It will be fun, don't worry."

"I trust you," he says, patting my leg. "I've got a couple of things in mind, too, but I'm not sure if we'll be able to make them happen with the twins here. I'm not sure what you're thinking, but I think they're a little young to take up skiing."

I pretend to consider the idea. "Really? I think they're about ready," I joke.

Alex chuckles. "Maybe next year. I do wish we could go, though. It seems a shame to come to Aspen and not ski."

I'm not bothered by the lack of skiing in my life, but I do feel bad that Alex has to miss out. I'm about to suggest that he and Dad take a trip to the slopes when Margaret butts in, sounding for all the world like a sweet grandmother.

"Well, I could watch the twins, of course. A young married couple needs some time alone after they have kids, don't you agree, Alex?"

"Yes…" he says reluctantly, noticing that I've set my fork down at Margaret's suggestion. "But, Mom…"

"Nonsense. Don't argue. Go with your wife and unwind a little. Petra looks like she could use some relaxation."

"Hey!" I start, but Alex talks over me.

"It's not a decision I can make myself. We only usually leave them with our nurse, Lily," Alex explains. I could groan when he looks over at me, a smidgen of hope for alone time in his eyes. "What do you think, Petra?"

I close my eyes, gathering my thoughts. My immediate response would be *Hell. No.* but if I draw too stark of a line in the sand, Margaret will surely see that I'm on to her and Catherine. If I want to find out the truth, I'll need to play it cool.

"I don't like it," I grit out. "But okay, once or twice would be fine. You can't leave the villa with them though!"

"Of course not," Margaret says, her tone suggesting I'm being ridiculous even hinting that she'd leave with them. "I'm not gonna be out in the freezing cold, pushing a double stroller on my own."

Alex is over the moon. I can see on his face how happy he is to be able to spend some couple's time with me, and I hate to rain on his parade. If he and I can get away for a little while, maintaining the facade of knowing nothing about the Margaret and Catherine connection, all the better.

His large, warm hand settles over mine and his thumb sweeps over my knuckles. It melts my heart a little to make him happy. I look over at my twins to see that Margaret has finished feeding them and is wiping their faces with a soft linen. Full to the brim of squash, sitting in front of the roaring fire, the twins are as content as I've ever seen them.

Realizing I'm the last one with food on my plate, I resume eating, the ravioli only a little colder than when I'd initially been served. I wish life was as simple as it seems to be right now; a loving mother and father and a doting grandmother, but I know something is lurking under the surface that I just haven't figured out yet.

Sweeping up the remainder of the pasta sauce with a piece of crusty bread and popping it into my mouth, I can at least rest assured that we won't starve during this trip. Everything else is still up in the air.

CHAPTER 4

Aspen, December 23, 2021
Petra Van Gatt

It's a bright and early eight a.m. the next morning, no clouds hanging in the sky, just sunlight reflecting off of the crisp, white snow. Inside our villa, I'm zipping the twins into their bunting coats, making sure their fingers are covered by the built-in gloves and adjusting their hats while Alex finishes his coffee at the breakfast bar. Margaret is reading a book in the living area, apparently enjoying the impressive view out the large bay window.

"You should come with us, Mom," Alex offers for the second time, to which Margaret shakes her head again.

"I'm going to stay in, I'm just not interested in the gondola ride."

I'm sure her disdain for the activity stems from the fact that I had planned the gondola ride myself, but I'd not give her the satisfaction of acknowledging it. I'll definitely enjoy everything more if she isn't present.

Alex sets his now-empty coffee cup on the marble counter and sighs, pinching the bridge of his nose between his fingers. "The whole reason you wanted to come to Aspen was to spend time with Jasmine and Jasper, but now you've decided you don't want to leave the house?"

"The tourist attractions just don't interest me, Alex. I'll join you for your next outing." She waves her hand dismissively towards him, never looking up from her book. I see Alex's jaw tense and wonder if this is a small glimpse into what his childhood had been like.

"Suit yourself!" I hear him saying as I look at the twins finally ready. Their coats are so thick that they're having a little more trouble moving than usual, and if their pinched, annoyed expressions are anything to go by, we need to get on with the entertainment before they decide they are done with the outdoor wear. Jasmine's coat is a soft heather purple and Jasper's a diluted gray.

Alex looks like he wants to say something more, but he snaps his mouth shut and takes their stroller to the car, deciding to abandon the disagreement with his mother, to my relief. I give the back of Margaret's head a jaunty wave as we leave, feeling lighter already as I close the door behind me. Good riddance!

***

In this area of town, people dressed casually were mixed pretty evenly with the skiers and snowboarders making their way from slope to slope. We aren't the only ones out with kids, but it's pretty clear what most people are in Aspen for: The winter sports.

Despite the focus on skiing and snowboarding, everything is decorated for Christmas, with long ropes of pine needles bedecked with red bows wrapping themselves around every light pole and fence post. I thought we'd beat the rush by leaving so early, but I couldn't have been more wrong. I guess skiing is an early morning extreme sport.

The twins seem to have gotten used to their huge snowsuits and are looking around with wide, curious eyes as we push them on their stroller towards the gondola. Sitting straight up in their seats, they get a full view of everything going on around them, and more than a few other pedestrians stop to give them little finger waves, gaining joyful giggles from Jasmine and more reserved chuckles from her brother. Between the bright outerwear everyone has on, the glittering snow, and all the splendid holiday decor, there is something for them to gawk at in every corner. It is certainly enough to distract them from not being able to put their arms all the way down.

Alex peeks over the hood of the stroller to look at his daughter. "Why do they look like starfish in these snowsuits?"

I scowl, fighting the urge to laugh. He isn't wrong. "Because they're the warmest coats that I could find."

Jasmine looks back at her father and grins, barely able to turn in his direction because of the puffy coat. "Well," Alex says, "they're certainly warm. That's all I'm going to say on the matter."

"Hey! The coats are cute!" I insist.

"No comment," Alex replies, miming zipping his lips and throwing away the key.

It's only a few blocks to the Silver Queen Gondola, and I expected it to be frigid out, but I'm pleasantly surprised at how much the buildings on either side cut down on the wind chill. That, combined with the shining sun, makes it a pleasant winter morning, all things considered. We could have driven, but I've been dying to check out the surrounding shops, so after the gondola ride, I'm hoping to tempt Alex into some retail therapy.

In the plaza where the loading dock for the gondola is located, we meet up with Dad and Catherine, the latter of which is dressed in enough mink fur to make me curl my lip in distaste. I'm not one to preach my vegan lifestyle on others, but I can't help wondering how many innocent animals were killed to make her long coat.

Alex and Dad do the typical manly handshake-hug combo, while I give Catherine a tense smile in place of the warm greetings everyone else is exchanging.

"Nice to see you," I tell Catherine, my tone hollow.

"Same to you, dear," she responds distractedly, bending over to look at the twins in their strollers. "My my," she comments. "Your mother certainly overdressed you two, didn't she!"

I want to grind my teeth. How did I get trapped on this vacation with not one old harpy in Margaret, but now two with Catherine included! I keep my false smile plastered on as I answer her. "They're preemies. They get colder easier. But thanks."

Catherine shrugs delicately. Feeling my eyelid beginning to twitch from stress, I turn to my dad and accept his warm embrace, happy for some honest-to-goodness genuine affection and not the cold, glib phrases I had been getting my fill of lately.

"Thanks for booking a gondola at the ass-crack of dawn!" Dad says with a laugh, patting me on the shoulder. "I'd hate to sleep in on my vacation."

"Glad I could help," I reply. "You can thank your granddaughter, though. Eight a.m. is basically noon for her, so I was just going by her schedule."

"An early riser, eh?" Dad asks Jasmine, who is making grabby hands at him to be removed from the stroller. "That will be an exceptional quality to have when you and your brother take over the company."

"Already thinking about that?" I ask, teasingly. "Why not let them decide when the time comes?" I don't like the idea of my children being stripped down of any choice like my dad tried to do with me. Only time will tell what they want to do later on, but I hope Dad and Alex both know that Jasper and Jasmine will have their choice in lifestyles once they are grown. CEOs, biologists, philosophers, or anything in between, they will have the choice to follow their dreams.

Alex checks his watch, shaking his wrist so he can see the face. "I think we'd better get going unless we want to wait in line with everyone else. Separate gondolas or one?"

Separate, please, separate, I think frantically, but my dad responds, "One, of course. I want to see my grandchildren's faces when we go up. No point in Catherine and I riding alone."

I pout as we enter the boarding building. There are two lifts stemming from this plaza; a traditional ski lift on my right and the Silver Queen Gondola on my left, which ends in a black glass building where the gondola cars slide through to let riders embark and disembark. They're enclosed, and warm enough from the sun reflecting off the shining surfaces and glass, but it's a tight fit for four adults. We park the strollers outside the building, Dad carrying Jasmine and Alex carrying Jasper, who has his arms tightly linked around his dad's neck as he silently takes in everything new and exciting around him.

There isn't much time to waste, since the gondolas are constantly in motion as they make their way up and down Aspen Mountain, so we board quickly when the attendants motion us over. Dad and I hop into the swinging car first, followed by Alex and Catherine. Alex sits next to me and across from Catherine, while I sit across from Dad, so we can all have the maximum amount of knee room in the tiny gondola.

We start to move with a hard jerk before swinging around and back outside into the daylight; the gondola is climbing the metal cord that it is attached to with ease. Surrounding us outside are hundreds of skiers and snowboarders, moving around casually, as if they were born with their skis and boards attached, all of them dressed in rainbows of colorful gear that pop on the bright white snow.

The ascent is timed to be about fifteen minutes, and I have to admit, the view is even better than in my memory. Downtown Aspen gets smaller and smaller as we climb, and the slope becomes heavily forested, besides the open swath of snow for the skiers.

Jasmine presses her gloved hands against the glass, leaning over Dad while he holds her for balance. Her warm breath fogs the glass as she leans close, fascinated by the world passing by outside and completely unbothered by the clunks and clanks when the gondola passes over the junctions of the towers.

Jasper is more reserved, keeping himself firmly pressed into Alex's arms while he observes everything. Alex scoots as close to the window as he can, letting Jasper gaze his fill from the safety of his arms. My babies… they're so similar yet already so different personality wise. Jasmine has been a warrior since the beginning, and her brave, fighter spirit remains, showing itself in everything she does. She will need her cool, collected brother to keep her grounded when she's older. They'll be the perfect team.

We rise into the air, snow kicked up by the wind glittering like diamonds in the surrounding air.

"It's different to look at this place without there being a rush to ski down the mountain," Dad muses as his granddaughter slaps handprints on the clean glass. "It's good to slow down."

Catherine leans her blond head on his shoulder, a blissful look on her face. *Gold digger,* my brain hisses, but I keep it to myself. I can only hope my theory about Catherine is wrong, but there's just too many coincidences.

"Are we disembarking at the top, or riding all the way back down?" Alex asks me quietly.

"We'll stop for some photos," I tell him. "I'd like to make family photo albums of all of our trips. Like with real, physical pictures. Not just the digital ones on our phones."

Alex squeezes my knee with his free hand. "Sounds perfect."

I don't have any time to bask in the quiet moment between my husband and me before Catherine raises her head from my dad's shoulder and taps him on it with a white painted fingernail. "Roy?"

"Yeah?" he answers absentmindedly, giving all his attention to Jasmine.

"Can I hold her?"

I snort, biting my lip so I don't giggle. *Good luck, lady. Should have asked for Jasper.*

I get it, really I do. Jasmine is irresistible, a six-month-old with her huge cerulean eyes and fluffy brown hair, but she is decidedly not an easygoing baby if she isn't down for whatever is happening. And strangers holding her is not on Jasmine's list of "things I enjoy."

"Uh, sure," Dad says distractedly, turning to hand Jasmine to his girlfriend. Jasmine balks at the offer, recoiling from Catherine's grasp and filling the gondola with an ear-piercing shriek. Catherine jumps, and her hands fall down to her sides.

"I guess that's a no!" I tell her with a sarcastic shrug. Catherine frowns, sinking back into her seat and saying nothing.

Alex gives me the smallest pinch on the knee, and when I look at him to frown, I see he has the same amused look on his face I do. I guess we're both proud of our little princess for holding strong to her boundaries.

***

Stepping out of the gondola, I stagger a few steps before catching my balance, unprepared for how fast the car was still moving. Everyone else gets off without a hitch, and I wait for my husband so we can walk out onto the pavilion together.

With the air being much brisker up here, I pull my gloves from my pocket and pull them on as I look around the place, taking in all the views.

"Anything specific you wanted to see while we're up here?" Alex asks, wrapping an arm around my waist.

I shake my head. "Nothing specific, I just wanted to check everything out."

It's clear that this area is mostly for skiers, and there probably isn't much to occupy a family of four—besides taking in the scenery. The only must-visit place on the summit is The Sundeck Restaurant, where a heated outdoor tent sits right on the precipice of a cliff overlooking everything.

"We're gonna go look around a bit," I tell Dad, who hands me Jasmine. "You two don't have to wait for us, you can head to the restaurant and get started. I made a reservation."

As much as I look forward to having breakfast with my dad, I can't say the same about his female companion, who is already eyeing The Sundeck with considering eyes, her hand placed on her hip.

"Yes, that sounds nice, actually. See you later then," Catherine says, having decided.

"Okay. Awesome," I grit out. I wait until she turns back to ask my dad something before rolling my eyes. Alex takes notice, threading his fingers with mine and pulling me away to explore.

"Come on, grumpy girl. Let's see what there is to see," he tells me placatingly.

I let myself be led away, but I can't hold hands with Alex for too long before I need both of my arms to support Jasmine's weight. Soon I'll have to break out the chest carriers for them if I want to carry them anywhere!

"I have to say," Alex muses. "For a self-proclaimed introvert, I'm impressed that you reserved both an activity AND a meal for us."

I brighten under his praise. "I talked to strangers on the phone and everything. Can you believe it?" I comment jokingly.

"Such bravery," he adds before stopping, pointing out a quiet area with an empty stone bench overlooking the valley. "How about there for some family pictures?"

"Perfect!" I exclaim.

I spend the next ten minutes adjusting hats, wiping runny noses, and making my two less than thrilled children as happy as can be before quickly posing Alex, both babies now in his arms, on the bench. Alex had been wearing our backpack-style diaper bag, and I stash it behind a small tree for safekeeping.

"Aren't you going to be in the pictures?" he asks as he wrangles the two squirming infants.

"Yes, yes, just give me a second."

Setting my phone in the crook of a sapling pine growing eight feet away from the overlook, I make sure the bench and its occupants are perfectly centered and focused. I rush to turn the timer on and hustle as quickly as I can to sit down next to Alex.

"Three, two, one," I murmur. "Smile!"

I can hear the clicks of the burst of pictures being taken, and I hop up to see how chaotic they have turned out. I had set my photo app to take a burst of twenty photos in two seconds, and out of all of them, 4 have the twins looking forward with their eyes open and Alex and I both smiling. It's not perfect, but it's endearingly adorable. I save them, clearing the failures.

"A success!" I tell Alex cheerfully, taking Jasper from him. Alex's hair and collar are both a little out of place from holding both babies and their four seeking, curious hands, but he is full of patience as I snap more pictures.

Some are just of Alex and the kids, some I have him take of just the kids and I, and I even lay myself flat on the ground while Alex sets the twins in the snow, letting them slap at the white fluff while I take candid shots of them with the spectacular view in the background.

Eventually, a good Samaritan sees our shenanigans and comes over, offering to take the pictures for us. I gleefully agree, and we add some standing, much more organized shots to our collection. I thank the older man profusely and pocket my phone after checking the time.

"It's about time for brunch," I proclaim, sweeping up our diaper bag from the snow while I balance Jasmine on my hip. The cobblestone pavilion is alive and bustling, even this high up, but the cold is turning the twins' cheeks and noses red, so it's a relief to step into the warmth of The Sundeck and be led to our table on the heated patio.

Dad and Catherine are waiting for us patiently, Catherine enjoying a cappuccino. Alex and I don't even bother getting high chairs. I simply hand Jasmine to Dad and pop their formula bottles into the heating cups inside the diaper bag, letting them warm while we wait.

"You two see anything interesting?" I query, to which Catherine sniffs disdainfully.

"Not unless you count a ski shop interesting."

A quick chuckle escapes me. I definitely didn't see her comment coming and refrain myself from shaking my head at it. Turning my attention to the waiter, I order a cup of orange spice hot tea once he comes by, and Alex goes for an espresso, and we all share an appetizer of various offerings. There's no time for a proper meal, with Alex and I feeding bottles to the twins, stripped out of the confines of their buntings and happily cradled in our laps. Conversation is stilted, as I had expected it would be, but I don't really mind. As much as I'd like to spend more time with my dad today, I'm more than happy to shed Catherine and the negative energy she brings.

"Petra," Catherine says airily, picking at an edamame pod. "I suppose I should invite you to the spa with me after we take the gondola back down. I know I could use it after all of this skin-drying cold air."

Uh, absolutely not. "Oh, I'd love to go, but we've got a few more things to do today. Maybe another day we can?"

She raises a single shoulder in a shrug. "Suit yourself."

I wonder what she could want from spending one-on-one time with me? Probably planning on getting me relaxed and asking some probing questions to see how open I'd be about Dad. No way, lady.

Once the babies are fed, their eyes start to become heavy, and I zip them into their coats before they're completely asleep and I can't get their limp arms and legs into the sleeves and pants. Dad pays the bill, and we make our way back to the Silver Queen Gondola. It's only 11:30 a.m., and there's a lot of day left in front of me. I plan to make the best of it.

And truthfully, had Catherine not been going to the spa, I definitely would have found my way there sometime today. Oh well.

The trip down the mountain is much speedier, with the gondola occasionally moving fast enough to make my heart rate pick up. Of course, I know it only feels so fast because we're up so high, but still, yikes.

I almost groan in relief when I set Jasmine, who is working her way to a nap, down in the stroller. My arms ache from carrying her for so long, but the sleepy grin she gives me as I lay her seat back in the flat position makes the workout worth it.

"You're too cute for your own good," I tell her, running a finger over her soft cheek.

"She certainly is," my dad says from behind me. "Just like her mother, of course."

"You flatterer," I laugh, slapping his arm jokingly.

"Thanks for inviting us today," he says, pulling me in for a quick hug. "It was nice, we enjoyed it."

I raise my eyebrows, and he laughs self-consciously.

"Okay, okay," Dad continues. "I enjoyed it, at least. But listen Petra, I can tell you and Catherine are a bit antagonistic towards each other. I hope it will fade in time, when you get used to her, and she gets used to all of us as a family. Just try to be a little happy for me, okay?"

"Mm-hmm," I say, unconvinced and full of trepidation from my suspicions about Catherine's actual intentions. "Just be careful, Dad. I like this new you. I don't want Catherine messing that up for us. Or you getting hurt."

"I can handle myself, I promise," he tells me, shoving his hands in his pockets. "We'll see you later, darling daughter. Have a good afternoon."

"You too, Dad," I tell him, watching him retreat to link arms with Catherine and head for the spa. I stare at them departing for a minute too long, causing Alex to sidle up next to me.

"Having trouble with Roy's new flame, huh?" he asks me, pulling me close so I can lay my head on his shoulder.

"It's more complicated than that…" I sigh. *It IS complicated*, I think. But I could still be wrong. Part of me really hopes that I am, so Dad can have this little slice of happiness.

"So, master planner," Alex says, breaking the tension. "What's next on the agenda?"

I shake my melancholy attitude off and give him a mischievous grin. "Clear your schedule, buddy, because we're going *Christmas shopping.*"

***

It's noon, and the kids are passed out, so Alex and I take this opportunity to go downtown and get some last minute Christmas presents for our friends and family. I rub my hands together gleefully as we head to the small vintage shops with unique items. Closest to us is The Little Nell Boutique, and it looks perfect for our first stop. The display windows are filled with wintery goodies: fluffy jackets, tall leather boots, and cape-style ponchos in shades of Aztec red and blue.

Inside, the heat is welcome, but it soon becomes stifling in my heavy winter gear, so I strip my coat off and tuck it in the mesh basket under Jasmine's stroller. She's still snoozing away, but I take the opportunity to tug her hat off and undo a few of the buttons on her jacket, hoping the change in temperature won't wake her.

The shop is carpeted with cream Berber, with dozens of handcrafted items on shelves and hangers. It's one of the many upscale boutiques in the area, and it definitely gives off the "luxury" vibe. There aren't any pressing crowds or loud tourists, for which I'm utterly thankful.

Alex goes off to browse on his own, no doubt thinking about all the other places he'd rather be and how many ski slopes he's going to drag me down for forcing him to come on my shopping spree. Thankfully, his gift is already on the way, and should arrive tomorrow according to the tracking on my phone, that I may or may not have checked over twenty times over the last few days.

Shopping today there are only a few people I'm looking to buy for: Emma, Dad, Matt, Lily, and a few extra things for the twins. They're at the age where the wrapping paper is going to be the most entertaining part of the gift, but it doesn't matter to me. I still want them to have plenty of things to open and for their first Christmas to be wonderful.

In New York, this would be a store I frequented often, but faced with the decisions of buying for others besides myself and the twins, my brain feels a little mushy. I'm out of practice when it comes to social gifting, but I must persevere.

Okay, I swear I'm here to buy other people's gifts, but the poncho from the window is calling my name. After only a few moments of hesitation, I slide over to the display and shrug the cape off the mannequin. The fabric is thick and warm on the outside but lined with soft fleece inside, and it stands out sharply from the creams and neutrals of the other items in the store with its brick red and turquoise chevron pattern.

The saleswoman at the front gives me an amused look and cocks an eyebrow as I whip it around me to settle in on my shoulders with a contented sigh.

"I'll wear it out," I tell her, and she nods, tapping a few keys on her computer.

Poncho acquired, I firmly focus on my Christmas shopping. Annoyingly, I realize that with Margaret staying with us in the villa, I'll have to buy her a gift, too. Oh well, something nice and generic will work just fine for her.

There's something special in the atmosphere this time of the year, and everyone I pass in the quiet aisles stops to say something kind about the babies or to show me some item that just can't be passed up. It's a far cry from the insanity that is Christmas in Manhattan, where it's almost a physical fight to get down the sidewalks and into the best stores. It seems everyone in Aspen is on the same page about how the holiday should really feel, and it gives me a fuzzy feeling inside.

Riding the high of that feeling, I take a kind older woman's advice on a locally made goat's milk soap and lotion combo scented with lavender, adding it to my order for my mother-in-law. If anyone could use some lavender, it's Margaret, the most uptight woman alive.

I waffle for a while on what exactly to get Lily. On one hand, it seems a little strange to buy my children's nurse, and my former doula, a gift, but on the other hand, she's almost become part of the family over these past few months with how often she's with us. I ask one saleswoman for advice, and she directs me to a selection of delicate glass bead bracelets, and I immediately decide on a jade one with a tree of life pendant on it.

I've almost decided to move on to the next shop when I spot my first perfect gift. On one of the glass shelves is a set of carved marble chess pieces, the stone hewn roughly to create a blunt and striking version of the traditional chess shapes. I stand on my tiptoes to grab the small box full of the pieces, turning them this way and that in my hands. The marble is cold and smooth, the white pieces shot through with gold flecks while the black pieces are as solid and dark as night. They're perfect for Matt, and I clutch them to my chest with happiness. One friend down.

Aspen is known for a few different kinds of shops. Ski and snowboard shops are obviously the most prevalent, followed by the high-end boutiques and clothing stores, but after that the scene is completely owned by two factions: antiques, and thrift shops. Emma is a big fan of vintage items from high-end brands, especially when she can score some limited editions, but it isn't my scene. So, after checking out at The Little Nell, we make a beeline for the famous Daniel's Antiques.

This isn't the stuffy, overly stocked antique store I'm used to, that's for sure. Everything looks flawless and is displayed elegantly. There aren't any boxes of records to sort through or Ziploc bags of costume jewelry; only the best antiques are here. I'm almost nervous about pushing the strollers through the place, terrified of knocking something priceless over with an errant turn.

Alex is immediately drawn into a conversation with the cashier, pointing out a watch or a compass or something, and talking in hushed tones. He's parked Jasper's stroller next to him, and I can see that our son is still happily napping. I shrug and leave him to it, on the prowl for something for Emma.

The thing is, I don't know *what* exactly I'm looking for. Like the chess pieces, I want the gift to jump out at me. I want it to be personal rather than expensive, though in this shop I suspect it will have to be both.

I tuck Jasmine's blanket around her a little tighter and peruse, her little snores bringing a smile to my face as I do so. It's really an incredible shop, almost like a museum, and it makes me wonder what the previous owners of these items would think of them being here, scrubbed clean and marked up to outrageous prices.

I consider quite a few different things for Emma, but none of them seem to fit right, until I spot a glass display case full of antique books. I'm not sure how much Emma reads these days, but I'm just too curious not to take a look. On the shelf right in front of me is a dark-brown, leather-bound book, with yellowed pages and bits of the leather curling on the edges of the spine. Emblazoned in gold letters on the cover is *Edgar Allan Poe: The Complete Tales & Poems*. It's clearly an old copy, and it reminds me of back in High School when "The Raven" was the only piece of literature Emma actually cared enough to read. We had spent a ton of time analyzing that poem together, and I guess Poe is the only poet she ever enjoyed. That should make the perfect souvenir for my best friend.

I go up front to ask the cashier to unlock the case for me, but Alex stops me before I can ask.

"Petra, I know you wanted to pick out the gift for your dad, but can I make a suggestion?"

"Sure," I tell him. He's almost vibrating with excitement, and I wonder what he's found for Dad. Alex rarely wants to participate in overly sentimental things, so I'm surprised he's so invested.

The sales associate, wearing white gloves, carefully takes a watch from the case. From what I can tell, it's solid gold, from the face to the band. The man holds it gingerly, bringing it up high enough that I can get a decent look at it.

"A 1977 vintage Rolex with Jubilee band, miss," the sales associate informs me.

I blink a few times, taken aback. "Alex, this must be insanely expensive."

"It can be from all four of us," he explains, waving at the sleeping babies in the strollers.

I shake my head. "I can't get my dad a Rolex, Alex! I'll never be able to top that in the future."

"We'll take it," Alex tells the sales associate, who looks like he's so happy he could faint.

I start to argue, but then think better of it. Dad is Alex's friend too, after all. Maybe this is Alex's way of smoothing over all the drama of the past year, and it will be a gracious gesture to show how much our reconciliation means to me. I blow out an exasperated breath, looking at the sales associate.

"Add Poe's book on the tab, too."

The sales associate holds his hand to his heart, seeming to hardly believe his luck. He'll certainly be getting a good commission.

They carefully fold everything in paper, the watch placed in an equally vintage case, while they wrap Poe's book in a long piece of white silk for safe keeping. I feel a little bizarre tucking such precious items into the bottom of the stroller, so we tip the sales associate a little extra to have the items delivered back to the villa.

After leaving Daniel's Antiques, we have a single stop left on my agenda: A small children's shop on the corner, the display filled with brightly colored toys and clothing. The twins are rousing, and they quietly take in the rainbows and glitter of the place as we stroll through.

I can't wait until they're older, and I can hold their little hands and bring them to a special place like this to pick out anything they want, but for now I need some gifts that are appropriate for them at their current age.

I find exactly what I'm looking for in the back of the shop. There's a display of handmade children's stuffed toys with no problematic buttons or small pieces that the babies could get in their mouths. They're small enough for them to hold, without being so small they would be easily lost. When I pick one up, they're soft and irresistibly squishy. A lovely souvenir from our first family vacation together. I pick out an arctic fox for Jasmine, and an owl for Jasper in honor of his famous wide-eyed stare. Paired with faux fur blankets in complementary colors, I'm more than satisfied.

"Are we finally finished?" my husband says playfully, looking up from wiggling a toy in front of Jasper's fascinated face.

"I think so," I say, equally relieved and bummed out. It seems like a waste to only have made it to three stores, but maybe I'll get some spare time later to check some more out.

Alex is relieved and I'm even a little surprised he doesn't jump and click his heels when we leave the store.

"I'm pooped," I tell him. "Let's go back to the villa and chill out in front of the fire."

"Absolutely, just let me check on one thing," he replies, pulling out his phone before scowling and muttering, "seriously?" under his breath.

"What is it?"

He closes his eyes and scrapes a hand through his hair. "What if we eat here?" he asks, out of the blue. "There's a really good French place called The Wild Fig that has a huge vegan menu."

My lips twitch into a smile at his suggestion. After all, eating out would mean avoiding Margaret for two out of three meals today. I nod.

"Okay, sounds great."

CHAPTER 5

Aspen, December 23, 2021
Petra Van Gatt

The Wild Fig is smaller than I expected, but the atmosphere is close and intimate. I still think I would rather be back at the villa, especially how over it the twins seem to be with their long day out, but I'll try to trust Alex and his judgment.

It's only early evening, but at this time of the year, the sun sets early, and it's already creeping low on the horizon, casting long shadows. We'd taken the car, none of us up for walking all the way to the restaurant, and luckily the place was empty enough that we were seated immediately.

After strapping Jasmine into the provided highchair, one of her blankets rolled and tucked behind her for stability, I sink exhaustedly into my own chair, resting my elbows on the pristine white tablecloth.

"The sun setting so early is really messing with me," I comment. "I'm so tired and I have no reason to be!"

"It has been a busy day," Alex says absentmindedly, flipping through his menu. I notice he continues to check his phone every few minutes, and it makes me a bit suspicious, but I push the feeling to the side.

"Sure, but a day like this wouldn't normally tire me out so quickly," I reply, perusing the options for myself and checking out the specials scrawled on a mirror hanging over the bar.

Alex looks up from his menu, giving me a serious look. "Are you getting enough protein? Iron?" he queries, eyebrows drawn together.

I blow out a breath. Ever since my close brush with malnutrition during my pregnancy, Alex has been overly observant about my health and eating habits. Part of me wonders if it's because he feels guilt from how thin and distressed I had become when he was living elsewhere.

"You have nothing to worry about," I assure him, reaching across the table to lay a hand over his. "I'm taking all my vitamins. Promise."

Mollified, Alex nods. I look over at Jasmine, who is blowing bubbles and concentrating extraordinarily hard on crumpling the kid's menu that was hilariously set in front of her as if she could read it and pick out her meal. She's occupied, though, so I leave her to it.

Jasper is taking his surroundings in, kicking his chubby legs as he does so. Both kids are well behaved for the moment, but I'm afraid hunger and fatigue are going to overwhelm them soon enough.

We've got a jar of the food that Lily packed in the diaper bag, but when the twins are overly tired, all they seem to want is formula. I hope they'll be in a good enough mood to accept the baby food, but there's no telling with this mercurial pair.

Our server is a curvier woman in her late twenties with a short, jet black bob and red lipstick. She welcomes us warmly, but really lights up when she greets the twins, bending over so she's at eye level with each of them. Her face is kind, but I think I can see the shadow of tiredness lurking behind her public facade. After introducing herself as Sharon, she helps me look over the menu and points out all the vegan options, plus what they can easily change to be made vegan.

"We don't get many little ones in here," she tells us conversationally as she takes our order. "It's mostly older couples without kids or the younger couples that are always on adult-only getaways."

We order, and I'm happy for the chance to talk to Alex without an audience of parents or parents' girlfriends.

"Speaking of getaways, what other places do you want to take the twins to when they get older?" I ask Alex.

"Hmm," he says, considering the question. "Venice, absolutely, but not until they're older. I have a feeling we're going to be spending a lot of time at Disney World."

He seems less excited about the latter option, and I laugh. "Hey, don't be so grouchy about it. I've heard it's way more fun once you have kids."

"It better be," he grumbles. "Anywhere special you had in mind?"

"Once they're kids instead of babies, I'd *love* to take them to the Louvre," I breathe, already thinking about how exciting it will be to share the artwork there with them for the first time. I wonder if either of them will take up painting as I did as a child, or what other hobbies they might find. I promise myself that we'll give them all the opportunities possible to stretch their creative wings.

"Okay, new question," I say, leaning forward. "Based on their personalities right now, what will be their hobby when they grow up? Like how mine was oil painting."

My husband looks at our children. Jasper, his head lowered and double chin on display, is picking at the fibers on his blanket, while his sister is still overjoyed at the loud crackling noise her crumpled menu makes. Alex's mouth skews up in a smirk.

"Jasper will train show dogs, and Jasmine will be a fencing master," he answers finally.

I laugh loudly, taken off guard by his response. "Fencing! Dogs!"

Alex nods solemnly. "Mark my words, they will be masters in their fields."

I snort. "And what kind of dogs is Jasper going to be showing?"

Alex raps his finger on the table a few times as he thinks, before saying confidently, "Pembroke Welsh Corgi."

I have tears in my eyes from holding back my laughter at this point, highly amused at this silly side of Alex. "I was going to say golf and soccer!"

"Well," he hedges, "I guess we'll see in about ten years what they're passionate of."

Our food is hot and welcome; risotto for me and lobster ravioli for Alex. The twins both sit up straight in their chairs, and I wince at my lack of foresight. I should have fed them first. I crack open the jar of baby food, what looks to be a green bean and carrot puree, and attempt to feed them, but they're having none of it.

I'm not sure if it's the strange environment or how tired they are, but no amount of cajoling can make them eat, and within a few minutes I'm feeling frazzled by their fussing and fully aware that my pricy dinner is getting cold.

I clench my jaw, pinching the bridge of my nose in frustration. We should have at least swung by the villa for bottles or to feed the twins before trying to go out. I wave off Alex's attempts to assist me, both annoyed and angry at myself for the mistake.

Sharon swings by to inquire about the meal and, feeling defeated, I ask for mine to be packaged up. The server furrows her brow, looking over my fussy children. "I can do that, but can I try something else first?" she asks.

Confused, but willing to try anything at this point, I give her the go-ahead. She disappears into the back of the restaurant and comes back in a few minutes with two black ceramic bowls filled with something creamy looking with purple-brown swirls throughout it.

She sits the bowls down in front of me instead of in front of the twins, thankfully, because they're worked up enough that I'm sure they would bury their hands in the food immediately.

"It's fresh vanilla yogurt with a swirl of our fig jam. When I have to bring my son in before the daycare opens, it's his favorite snack. Always has been," Sharon tells us, her tone self-conscious. "I thought they might like it, too."

I don't eat yogurt, so I slide one bowl over to Alex, who takes a small spoonful. His eyebrows shoot nearly up to his hairline. "It's great, seriously."

Sharon gives us a nervous smile, twisting the string of her apron around one finger. "I hope I didn't overstep…"

"Not at all!" I assure her. "Thank you *so* much."

"Enjoy your meal," she says quickly, hustling off to the back of the restaurant.

Once the twins realize I'm not trying to feed them the veggie baby food anymore, they both tentatively accept the bite from my spoon, eating it happily and opening their mouths for the next serving immediately.

Thank goodness for Sharon's motherly instincts, because Alex and I are able to feed each baby in between bites of our food, and the meal goes much smoother than I had expected it to ten minutes ago.

I watch the server out of the corner of my eye as we eat. She seems to be the only one in the place besides the manager we spotted on the way in, and I wonder how much time she has to spend here, away from her young son. I chew my lip thoughtfully.

"Alex," I say, catching my husband's eye. "Let's leave her a little extra for a tip. It's Christmas time, after all."

The look he gives me is warm and sweet. "Sure thing, my soft-hearted wife."

"I'd be your empty-stomached wife if she hadn't found something they would tolerate eating."

The rest of dinner goes by without incident, and by the time we are finished, the sun is fully set, and I am full to bursting. I lean back in my chair with a groan. Thank goodness we took a car here, because there is no way I could walk back to the villa in this state.

Sharon, the server, brings the bill by, and when she walks away, letting us know she'd return for payment shortly, Alex sets his credit card on the slip of paper and slides it over to me to fill out the tip line.

I think about the gifts I'd bought my friends today, and how much I am looking forward to spoiling Jasmine and Jasper every single year of their childhoods for Christmas. Giving things to the ones I love makes me so happy…but writing a $100 tip for our server makes me happier still. Giving someone who is basically a stranger some extra money to spend on her child seems like the most Christmassy thing I could possibly do.

I push the card and paper back over to Alex to sign, and he doesn't even bat an eye at my choice in amount. I can see our server over near an order terminal, and once Alex is done signing, I motion for him to put his coat on.

"Don't you want to see her reaction?" he asks.

"It's not about that. Plus, it's almost a little embarrassing for me. I just want it to be a kind gesture. I don't need anything out of it."

Alex shrugs but puts on his coat and zips Jasper back into his. I follow suit with our daughter, a giddy feeling in my stomach. I don't necessarily want to be caught, so I rush us through our departure.

Alex has made it outside, but before I can get out behind him, I feel a tentative touch on my shoulder. I turn around to see Sharon, misty eyed, staring back at me.

"Thank you," she says simply. "It's been a rough year for us in these restaurants. Just… Thank you. Merry Christmas, ma'am."

I feel myself getting a little choked up as well, and I fan my face with my hand. "Merry Christmas to you too. Thank your son for his great yogurt recommendation."

She gives me a watery laugh and a nod. "I will. Have a good night."

I follow Alex to our ride, feeling light as air and absolutely awash in the Christmas spirit. Despite Margaret and Catherine, Aspen really has brightened my holiday so much. It's such a fresh setting compared to Manhattan, and the slower pace gives my soul a chance to rest and play catch up.

Alex doesn't ask me how it went. He just assists me in strapping Jasmine into the car seat in the back row alongside her brother, and when we take off, the lights in the car dimming, he pulls me close and kisses the top of my head. My eyes flutter closed as I snuggle up to him.

Back at the villa, Alex almost seems nervous as we unload the kids, who are full of yogurt and in need of a diaper change. He takes Jasmine's carrier from my hands when we reach the door and blocks my way in.

"Cover your eyes," he says, his voice tense with a hint of excitement.

"What are you up to?"

"Don't ask questions," he insists. "Just close your eyes."

With a heavy sigh, I follow his directions, covering my eyes with my hands and waiting patiently. Alex rings the doorbell, and after a few seconds I hear the door crack open. The elderly Earl greets Alex with a, "Welcome home, master Alex! Everything has been finished as requested, and the decorators have just departed."

"Shh," I hear him tell Earl, laughter in his voice. "Don't ruin my surprise, Earl."

"Apologies, sir."

I'm still covering my eyes, feeling the warmth from the seemingly always-lit fireplace at my front and the chill from the outdoors at my back. I hear Alex set down the car seats, returning to lead me gently inside and closing the door behind me.

"Open your eyes." he whispers.

My eyes pop open, and I gasp. Like I had anticipated, the enormous fireplace is blazing, my unamused mother-in-law sitting primly on the couch in front of it. The ridiculously immense pine tree is still there in the corner, reaching to the second floor to where I could touch it from the balcony at the top of the stairs. But that's all that remains the same.

The white lights and classy, matching ornaments and decor are gone. In its place are all the things Emma and I had bought back in Manhattan. It's a wash of uproarious color, the rainbow of lights twinkling and illuminating the otherwise conservative-looking villa. It must have been a colossal pain in the ass to have had it all shipped here and put up, but Alex had done it for me. He had *listened* when I lamented leaving my new decor behind and worked to give me this surprise.

I squeal in excitement, covering my mouth.

"It's absolutely garish," Margaret comments from the couch, not even bothering to look up from her book.

"I *know*," I breathe joyously, throwing my arms around my husband's neck. "Thank you so much!"

"Does this make up for bringing Mother?" he whispers in my ear, low enough so she can't hear it.

"No," I whisper back with a giggle, before pressing my lips to his.

He pulls away long enough to tell me, "It was worth a try," before we resume kissing beneath the brilliant tree.

CHAPTER 6

Aspen, December 24, 2021
Petra Van Gatt

A snowball, barely packed together, hits me in the temple and explodes into a million little pieces. My children, the little traitors, laugh uproariously as I scrape the snow off my face.

"Hilarious," I say dryly, looking at my dad, who has just decided to join us for our morning playing-in-the-snow session. He looks more like he should be enjoying a hot toddy in a lodge somewhere with his brown leather coat and scarf, and I'm sure he's not going to get on his hands and knees with the kids like I currently am, but I appreciate him joining us, nonetheless.

Well, I would if he wasn't tossing snowballs at me. If you had told me a few months ago that the one and only Roy Van Gatt would throw a snowball, I'd have guffawed, but having grandchildren can change a person, I guess. And if I've learned anything about babies, it's that the funniest thing on the planet to them is if anything inconveniences me at any given moment, snowballs included.

Aside from when it's hitting me in the face, I don't think the twins are huge fans of the snow. It was a novelty at first, and they had both greatly enjoyed using their mitten-clad hands to push and swish the snow this way and that, but after a few minutes, they seemed almost bored. Still, I wasn't going to miss out on letting them have every new experience possible here in Aspen.

Dad groans as he sits on the bench closest to the twins and me, his hands shoved in his coat pockets. "Merry Christmas Eve, you three. Any big plans on the agenda today?"

I shake my head. Alex had mentioned skiing the day before yesterday, but tomorrow was Christmas and the day after Margaret goes home, so if I can avoid her watching the kids, I will. Alex is inside, shut in our bedroom with his laptop out as he checks in on a few work ordeals, so I haven't gotten to pick his brain today about what we should get into.

Dad frowns. "You guys should do *something* while we are here! Even Catherine and Margaret went to the spa together yesterday. I guess it mended the fences." He jerks his head towards the patio.

Lounging at the outdoor table beneath one of the radiant heaters, Margaret and Catherine are drinking coffee and chatting under their breath to each other, looking for all the world like old friends. Thinking back to the argument at the coffee shop the other day, my suspicions are raised even further. Who becomes friends with someone they initially despised so quickly?

"Dad..." I start quietly. "I know you don't know Margaret all that well, but when have you known her to make such fast friends?" I ask, keeping a neutral tone.

My father watches the two older women for a moment too, his frown deepening when Margaret says something that makes them both laugh, eyes and noses crinkled.

Still, he seems to shake off the odd sight. "It is a little odd, but I'm not going to argue if the two of them want to get along instead of being at each other's throats. Makes my life easier, I'll tell you that much."

I exhale, pulling my attention away from the women and back to the twins. I can't bring my dad up to date on my theories yet, considering I have nothing to go on. "You're right," I admit, knowing it to be a total lie in my heart.

We chat a little more while I play with the kids, writing their names in the snow with my fingers and letting them slap them away, flakes flying into the air. It keeps them entertained for a while, but it isn't long until the cold outweighs the fun, and their laughs turn to grunts and babbles of annoyance.

"Fine, you little party poopers," I tell them, scooping them up into my arms. It's a chore to stand holding them both, but I manage.

Dad at least follows me to the door, opening it for me, but he doesn't join me inside. Instead, he takes a seat at the patio table under the heater with Margaret and Catherine.

Well, that's weird… but maybe he's catching on that the situation is a little strange and wants to get to the bottom of it himself.

Inside, the twins squirm in my arms, all but begging to be put down and their huge coats removed. I lay them down on the ottoman gently, trying to control them both while unzipping their coats. It's a colossal hassle, and when I manage to get one limb free from a coat, the other baby is trying to roll away.

I'm sweating and out of breath by the time I finish depositing them both in their playpen and wiping my forehead with the back of my hand. It's right then that Alex comes into the view, an apologetic look on his face when he sees how flushed I am and the scattering of baby winter gear all over the surrounding floor.

"Guess I'm too late to help you out. I'm sorry," Alex says with a wince.

"It's okay," I lie, wishing desperately for another set of hands for situations like these. "I managed."

Alex reaches the living area where we are and comes over to take my coat as I shrug it off, taking it to the closet while I busy myself by falling with a huff onto the couch. It's still morning, and I'm already beat!

When my husband returns, he holds my chin in one hand and examines my face, searching for something, but I have no idea what.

Finally, he says, "Let's get out of here and go to the slopes."

I thin my lips in a grimace. "You know we can't." I motion over to the playpen, where the twins are sitting on their bottoms and trying to fit shaped blocks into the correct holes in a hollowed out plastic circle.

"Mom will watch them," Alex insists, taking my hands and trying to pull me off the couch. "We just need to let her know that we're leaving."

I protest again. "She's probably got another spa day. She went yesterday with *Catherine* and apparently it was a blast."

"I don't care," Alex tells me, a stubborn look in his eye. "She offered, and now we're going to make her keep true to her word. Let's. Go. Skiing."

I nibble my lip nervously. It *would* be lovely to get out for a while, just the two of us, but if we let Margaret watch the kids today, then how much time is she going to demand with them in the future? If I give an inch, will she take a mile?

"Alex, I don't know..."

"Need I remind you that *you* also agreed to let her watch the twins. Don't make a liar out of us both, Petra."

I groan, scrubbing my hands over my face. Alex takes that as an affirmative, opening the patio door and yelling out. "Mom," he calls. "Come in here for a minute!"

Margaret wastes no time coming to Alex, desperate to see how best she can force herself into our business, I imagine. "Yes?" she asks, raising her eyebrows.

Casually, Alex tells her, "We're going out for the day, to the ski slopes. We'll be back tonight, okay?"

Margaret looks surprised, glancing down at the two kids in the playpen for a second before recovering herself. She *had* offered. No backing out now. It's not that I want her to watch them, but the idea of ruining any plans she had made brings me a smidgen of joy.

"Yeah," I add smugly. "We'll be gone *all* day, Margaret."

Her expression is pinched, but she eventually nods. "Of course! And don't worry," she adds. "Your father and Catherine will be at their villa all day today, so if anything goes amiss, I have backup right next door."

That actually does make me feel a little bit better. At least my dad had interacted with the twins over three times in their entire lives. "Okay, perfect."

Alex and I head to our bedroom to change into our ski clothes. White coat and scarlet pants for me. Alex's ski suit is a gunmetal gray top and bottom, a white stripe running the length of the set. My suit is brand new, and I rotate my neck in a circle a few times, feeling a little stifled. I shove matching red gloves in my coat pocket and braid my hair in two braids to keep it out of my face.

Looking at myself in the mirror, my stomach turns with mild anxiety. I look the part, but I haven't skied in so long that I'm a little worried about embarrassing myself in front of Alex, who seems to be good at every single thing he does. Well, whatever. I guess I'm out of luck if I can't remember what to do. It should be fun either way. If I'm dreadful, I'll just hang out in the lodge and drink hot cocoa.

I kiss the twins goodbye, feeling a little lump in my throat at leaving them with my mother-in-law. I know they'll be fine, and the time away will help me relax some, but I still don't love the idea of leaving them.

"Be good," I tell them, snuggling them close and breathing in their smell deep into my lungs. Jasper pats each of my cheeks, murmuring "ba ba ba" to me as he does, and Jasmine squeals to be released from the hug.

"Come on, Petra," Alex says, equal parts amused and annoyed at how long I'm taking. "They'll be here when we get back, I promise."

Swallowing hard, I square my shoulders and follow him out. He watches my face as we head to the SUV, silent until we are both buckled in. He'd started the vehicle remotely, and I warm my hands in front of the vent as he speaks.

"You're never this emotional about leaving them with Lily," Alex comments.

"Yeah, well, Lily is a nurse," I point out.

"You're still scared for them, aren't you? From how fragile they were after the birth?"

I sigh, closing my eyes. "You know I am. I probably always will be... You're nervous too. Remember the swim class?"

"Yes, but that was because it was an unfamiliar experience. You're afraid just leaving them alone with someone new, even someone that has raised children before, like my mother." Alex reaches over and squeezes my knee reassuringly. "This is all part of letting them be independent as they grow. If you can't leave them with their grandmother now, how will you ever leave them in kindergarten five years from now?"

I take a deep breath in through my nose and out through my mouth, letting Alex's words take away some of the uncertainty. Eventually I lay my hand over his and squeeze back. "You're right. I'm good. Let's go."

He grips my hand, raising it to his mouth and kissing my fingers. "How about a coffee first, tired girl? They have a maple and oat milk latte at the shop near the lift."

Oh man, he's really speaking my language now. "If you keep talking like that, you're going to have to get a hotel room instead of a set of skis."

With a chuckle, Alex pulls our vehicle out onto the road, driving carefully through the crowded downtown area. We're headed to the lift near the gondola from yesterday, but first we go and get our equipment. Even though it's still morning, this is a late start for skiing, and I have some serious catching up to do with figuring everything out.

Still, it's good to be going anywhere with Alex. I watch his handsome face as he drives us, the sparse sunlight making his stubble seem almost bronze on his cheeks. He's come a long way, my cold, aloof husband. He's becoming gentler and patient with me, and he's a more fabulous father than I could have ever imagined.

"I love you," I tell him out of the blue.

He glances at me quickly, a soft expression on his face before he looks back to the road. "I love you too, little Petra."

My wonderful Alex. I can only hope that he's as good a ski instructor as he is a husband, because if not, we might be in for a long day.

I'm *really* going to need that latte.

After Alex takes me to the coffee shop, and with my extra-large latte clutched between my hands, we go to the ski shop to get fitted. He actually had a set of skis at home, but with the babies, he had assumed he wouldn't get a chance to use them. Still, he doesn't seem to object to looking over the latest models, laser focusing on some black and silver Pro limited edition models, of course.

Just like at the antique store, I can almost see the dollar signs in the sales associates' eyes as he leads Alex throughout the store. I don't complain, taking the time to enjoy my coffee and looking over some of the more fashionable items.

I don't escape for too long, though. Eventually Alex has me sit in a chair while the associate fits me with the boots and skis. He has me walk in the boots first, and when he and Alex find them acceptable, he clasps the skis onto the boots. The salesman then explains us how these are great for both backcountry and resort skiing. "These skis are decently lightweight for climbing at 6 pounds 13 ounces, and have a great shape for smooth operation on the downhills. Plus they boast a premium construction that's built to last," he adds.

"Do you like them?" Alex asks.

"Uh, sure," I say, really having no idea what I'm looking for in a pair of skis.

After strapping a helmet to my head, shoving a pair of poles into my hands, and giving me a pair of reflective goggles, I guess that I'm ready to go. I drain my coffee, already mourning its loss, and follow Alex out to the lift.

Once outside, I push my boots into the skis until they click, sliding behind my husband as he leads me to where I need to go. I remember more than I thought I would, and don't have too much trouble locomoting. I'm even able to stop after going down a small decline, bringing the tips of my skis together so I can skid to a halt.

This makes Alex laugh. "The snow plough, huh?"

I scowl at him, lifting my goggles. "Yeah, so what?"

"Nothing," he cajoles, "I just didn't realize you were ten years old."

Alex demonstrates the parallel stop, spraying snow as he does. It's impressive and quick, but a little advanced looking for me.

"I'm good with the snow plough," I tell him.

"Suit yourself, newbie," he jokes, dodging the playful slap I aim at him, swooping towards the lift gracefully. I go with him, keeping a good pace, albeit not looking nearly as skilled.

Watching the ski lift, I hesitate. It's a long way up, holy moly. Looking longingly over at the gondola, I reluctantly follow my husband to the open lift and its lengthy climb.

We step up, falling back into our seats as soon as the bench touches the back of our calves. I squeak a bit, but

Alex's firm thigh pressing against mine reassures me, even as the lift pulls us higher and higher up the mountain.

"This is a lot of work for just skiing," I mention, kicking my feet to show all the gear we're now wearing.

"It will be a good time," he says with certainty. "I promise."

The lift is honestly terrifying, and I grip Alex's arm as we rise and rise, wringing a promise out of him that we'll take the gondola next time. The flattened ground of the top of the mountain is a welcome sight, and we dismount from the bench, skis landing in the snow with a "thump."

Alex bumps me with his elbow. "Well, now that we're here, let's get you up to speed, my love. Then we'll have some *real* fun."

I'm not sure how much I like the sound of *real* fun, but I force myself to be brave and go with my husband, putting my faith in him.

It turns out that relearning how to ski isn't nearly as chaotic as I thought it would be. Alex is patient and thorough, waiting until I gain some confidence in my balance and ability before taking me down the first bunny slope. At the first burst of speed, I grip my poles as tight as my gloves will allow, but I'm surprised at how much I'm enjoying myself!

By the time I meet Alex at the bottom of the hill, snow ploughing to a stop, my smile is wide enough that it hurts my cheeks. "Let's do it again."

Alex humors me, and we do the bunny slope again, and then a third time before he pulls me away to the larger hills. The first goes well, and I'm riding high on adrenaline when he takes me to the second slope. It's the first one I'm going to attempt that has any real steepness to it, but I'm confident. I've succeeded so far!

But I didn't succeed this time.

My fall isn't too dramatic, just a slow tumble when the front of one of my skis digs into the slope, but I still get a mouthful of snow before I can pick myself back up, face burning with humiliation.

Alex skids to a stop beside me, and after he checks me over, genuine worry laced in his eyes, he hauls me to my feet. Once he realizes I'm unharmed, aside from my pride, I can see the laughter pulling at the corner of his mouth.

"Don't you dare," I warn, and he turns away with a snort, quickly collecting himself.

Alex helps me brush the snow off myself, even ducking his head for a quick kiss. "Maybe backcountry skiing is more your style."

Well, I'm already wearing the skis, so why not?

Alex and I travel to the back trails, and I'm winded by the time we reach the more heavily wooded areas, but to my greatest surprise, here the slopes are slow and gentle, and I swiftly catch my breath. While the front slopes were crowded and boisterous, here, on the other side of the mountain Alex and I are nearly alone, just the sounds of the birds and the wind in the trees keeping us company.

The world is only three colors out here in the forest: the white of the snow, the brown of the tree bark, and the evergreen of the luscious pines. The beauty of this place soothes my soul.

"I like this," I tell Alex, almost in a whisper. "Like, a lot."

"I should have known you wouldn't be an adrenaline junkie," Alex replies, winking at me.

We talk little, just Alex giving me periodic directions. The shushing of our skis over the snow is almost hypnotic. It's been almost an hour, and to my dismay, I can see the trail curl off a way below us, leading back to the main area of the ski resort.

I'm about to ask Alex if there are any other off-piste terrain we can visit before heading back to the villa, but before I can open my mouth, he holds his pole up horizontally to the ground, stopping me in my tracks. I quickly bring the tips of my skis together and skid to a stop.

"Wha—" I start, but Alex shushes me.

"Shh…" he tells me, gesturing to our left with the pole. "Look behind the two trees there, down just a bit."

I follow his gaze and gasp softly. Standing in the snow, his head lowered to the ground as he paws for fresh foliage, is a bull elk, his antlers arching high above his enormous head. His coat is somewhere between buckskin brown and red, unblemished and stunning.

I can't find any words, both in awe of the immense creature and wondering how afraid I should be. Alex is stock-still, his spine rigid.

The elk looks up at us slowly, the steam of his breath curling around his nostrils as he snorts a few times. My heart is galloping in my chest, and I almost feel light-headed. The regal animal observes the two of us for minutes on end, as motionless as we are, but finally, he turns and makes his way through the woods, and eventually out of our sight.

I see Alex take a huge breath and exhale, and it sounds shaky to me. I feel the same, my insides like Jell-O, but I'm still floored by the experience. Wide eyed, I turn to face my husband, and we laugh quietly, both us of jittery and coming down from the high of the experience.

When Alex starts to move down the slope again, it's with a little more urgency. I follow, talking just to burn off some of the energy inside of me. "I can't believe what we just saw."

"It was dangerous as fuck," Alex responds. "A bull elk roaming freely…"

"He seemed nice enough."

I can't see Alex's face, but I'm willing to bet money that he is rolling his eyes at me. "You're ridiculous. Scared of skiing but totally comfortable with gigantic wild animals."

I smirk. "I have to say, skiing is the only one of the two that caused me to fall."

The trail leads us back to the major portion of the mountain, and back to the reality of all the other tourists and skiers. It's a whiplash change of pace from the quiet forest, and suddenly I decide I am over skiing for the day. Enough people, enough elks, and enough falling.

I say as much to Alex, who agrees. He's had enough of the slopes to satisfy him, and he's content to take us back to the lodge. Having purchased a premium membership to the lodge with our lift tickets today, Alex guides me past the bustling main part of the lodge to the elevators, which take us to the second floor reserved for members.

One would think I'd have had my fill of fireplaces by now, but the hulking round one in the center of the upper lodge calls me to it like a siren's song. I've long since removed my skis, but the plush leather sofa in front of the fire tempts me to remove my boots too, and within minutes I'm warming my nearly frozen toes in front of the flames.

We aren't the only ones here; about a dozen other members mill around, drinking their choice of hot beverage and chatting to one another. Alex had disappeared when he had gotten off the elevator, and he returns to me now, trading a kiss from me for a almond milk hot chocolate in a cardboard cup.

"Thank you," I groan, stripping my gloves off to absorb the heat coming through the cardboard.

He sits down next to me, and we warm ourselves together in companionable silence. I let my head fall to his shoulder with a sigh. "I'm going to need a foot massage when we get back to the villa."

He chuckles. "That's what the spa is for."

"That's what *husbands* are for," I correct him.

Alex takes a long sip of his own drink, tapping his fingers on the cup. "So, have I made a skier out of you?"

"No," I say instantly and then amend my statement with a "Maybe."

We leave the lodge as the sun sinks lower and lower in the sky, the early darkness coming on faster than we can anticipate. Alex stays true to his promise, and we ride the gondola down Aspen mountain, warm and cozy instead of freezing and exposed. It's almost fully dark when we emerge, stripping of most of our ski gear that a lodge employee loads into the SUV for us.

I can't believe we've actually been gone a whole day, especially on Christmas Eve, but I'm relieved to find no guilt in my heart. There are no frantic messages from Margaret on my phone, and I'm sure my babies are waiting for me back at the villa, warm and well fed.

We drive even slower than when we came in this morning, and I even roll down my window, listening to the roving packs of carolers as they make their way through downtown Aspen. It's almost something out of a dream, the a cappella Christmas songs weaving through the night air, paired with the festive lighting coming together to form something truly magical.

Margaret and the twins are indeed waiting on us when we come home, and I'm honestly surprised to see Jasmine contently held in her arms while Jasper snoozes in the playpen. I don't plan on waking them, but when I go to take my daughter from Margaret, there's a soft knock at the door. Carolers.

Oh well, it's Christmas Eve after all. The twins can stay up a little longer.

They're bleary-eyed as I wrap them in blankets, carrying them out onto the front balcony attached to the master suite. The air is frosty, and the babies wince when it touches their face, but their discomfort doesn't last long.

I'm not sure if they understand what all the singing is about, but at least eight carolers stand in the yard below, singing their hearts out.

"*On the first day of Christmas my true love gave to me...*"

Jasmine and Jasper are quiet, soaking in everything around them, listening almost studiously as the carolers sing. Alex, holding Jasper, comes close enough that we lean on each other, our children clutched in our arms and fat, lazy snowflakes falling around us.

It's late, it's cold, but it's wonderful.

CHAPTER 7

Aspen, December 25, 2021
Petra Van Gatt

Everyone has told me, over and over, that Christmas will feel different with children, and that Christmas with children will be just as exciting as when I was a kid myself, if not more so. I've learned not to put too much belief in everyone else's parenting experiences, because with kids, no one's experience is ever the same. But I can honestly say my first Christmas morning with Jasmine and Jasper is one of the greatest days of my life.

Our first Christmas together dawns bright and clear, a fresh dusting of snow having fallen the night before but all the clouds dissipating before dawn. I'm awoken by a beam of sunlight peeking through the curtains and landing directly on my face. Annoying at first, but once I realize what day it is, I'm up in a snap, shaking Alex's sleeping form until he groans from under the covers.

"It's Christmas," I plead, and with an unhappy noise, he sits up, his hair mussed from sleep.

"I'm up, I'm up."

It's only five a.m., and not even the kids are awake yet, so I slip into the shower and scrub myself clean with peppermint soap, winding my hair in a towel and tugging on my jeans. I pull a holly-green sweater from out of the armoire and don it before unwrapping my hair and turning the hair dryer on low, so as to not wake anyone else up.

Alex eventually joins me in the bathroom, showering himself without speaking, clearly still too tired to socialize. I have to wipe the mirror a few times, but eventually my hair is dried, and Alex gets out from under the steaming spray.

I'm momentarily distracted by the white fluffy towel slung low on his hips, and when I look back up at his face, there's a suggestive grin on his lips.

"Not right now," I insist, blushing. "After gifts!"

"Have it your way," he says with a shrug, voice gravelly with sleep.

I've just swept some mascara over my lashes when the movement monitor beeps, and the video feed from the baby monitors shows the twins rousing slowly, stretching their little bodies with enormous yawns.

They're soft and warm as Alex and I lift them from their cribs, both of us taking time to cuddle the drowsy infants, letting them press their cheeks and hands to our faces. We don't bother with a change of clothes, leaving them in their festive Christmas pajamas after a quick diaper change. I'm vibrating with giddy impatience as they drink their morning bottles, and when they finish, it's finally time to go downstairs.

Margaret, by far my least favorite part of this special morning, is wide awake and perfectly dressed, sipping her cup of tea as she eyes me disdainfully. I ignore her, texting my dad to come over as soon as he can.

I've barely taken my cup of matcha from Earl when the doorbell rings, and Alex lets my father and Catherine in from the cold. Dad's eyes are sparkling, his arms laden with gifts, but Catherine has the same snobby expression on her face that she always does. The only person she bothers to greet is Margaret, sitting right next to her enemy-turned-friend despite all the other seating in the room.

But, whatever. Even the two of them can't dampen my spirits. Everyone is here, and it's time for gifts.

I hold Jasper in my lap, sitting in front of the tree, the twinkling rainbow lights shining multicolored spots on his fair skin. Alex sits next to us with our daughter, and the grandparents (plus Catherine) rest on the couch, seemingly content to watch the chaos of children opening gifts from a little farther away.

Jasmine and Jasper are almost overwhelmed with the amount of things in front of them. Their eyes are as wide as saucers and glimmering with the different colored wrapping paper that they gleefully tear from the packages, with our help, of course. They hold each gift for a millisecond before discarding it on the ground and reaching for the next shiny thing they can get their hands on. It gives me a warm, fuzzy feeling inside when they spend a few extra seconds on the plushes I had found for them, rubbing their cheeks against the soft fur, babbling quietly to their new stuffed friends.

The living area looks like a war zone of wrapping paper and bows once they are done, and it's almost as good as having a babysitter to let the twins dig through the torn paper while the adults exchange gifts.

It surprises me to receive a gift from both Catherine and Margaret, but much less shocked when I open them to reveal a candle and a pair of wool socks, respectfully. I thank them with my teeth clenched but laugh to myself when they open their identical goat's milk soap presents from me.

Catherine's eyes bug out of her head when Dad unwraps his gift from Alex and me, holding the Rolex reverently in his hands before sliding it onto his wrist.

"This is incredible," he tells us, his voice suspiciously gruff. "Thank you both."

Dad gifted me a set of ethically sourced natural bristle paintbrushes, and a vintage fountain pen for Alex to display in the office. Alex bought his mother a black Tahitian pearl necklace, which she cooed over with more affection than I've seen her show her grandchildren. Now, everything else has been gifted, besides the large box marked for Alex from me, and the much smaller one from him to me.

We both hold our gifts in our laps, awkwardly telling each other to open theirs first.

"At the same time?" I suggest, and Alex nods.

"Three, two, one..."

We both tear into the paper, and with mine being so much smaller, I'm through the paper hastily. Inside is a red velvet jewelry box, which I open with careful reverence. These are our first gifts exchanged as parents!

Inside the box, resting on a pillow, is the most brilliantly clear diamond tennis bracelet I've ever seen, except the two stones directly in the center of the bracelets are a deep, dark blue, with hints of turquoise glimmering in the depths.

"Is this...?" I ask, my heart in my throat.

"Alexandrite," Alex answers, knowing my question without me even finishing it. "The twins' birthstone."

It's such a thoughtful, personal gift, and when fastening it onto my wrist I have to wipe a few tears from the corners of my eyes. "Thank you, Alex." I sniffle.

It's then that I realize he's opened my gift, too, and is holding the black peacoat in his lap, his thumb rubbing over one of the mother-of-pearl buttons.

"I have an idea what this is," he says warmly. "But why don't you tell me, just to be sure."

"It's... the buttons..." I clear my throat, still fighting back tears. "The buttons are made from mother-of-pearl from our honeymoon island. I had the coat tailor-made for you."

Alex leans forward, cupping my face in his hands and kissing me soundly. I close my eyes, hearing and feeling all the gratitude I would ever need from him through his lips on mine. It's a chaste kiss, but brimming with sentiment, and when we separate, the torrent of love between us doesn't abate.

"Merry Christmas," I tell him, my voice watery. I don't notice anyone else, just Alex and our children playing beside us.

"Merry Christmas to you too, wife."

***

All the high emotions and gift-giving behind us, we gather around the huge dining table for breakfast. Chef George, his permanent scowl fixed in place, serves us stacks and stacks of tender pancakes, fresh whipped cream, with multiple bowls of fruit on the side. Even the weirdness between Margaret, Catherine, and I seems to dissipate for the moment as we enjoy our family breakfast.

I continue to watch Margaret closely, though, her interactions with Alex especially. I'm not totally sure, but I feel like if I was an unbiased third party, they wouldn't look any different from any other mother and son duo. Margaret is usually aloof and distant, but it seems like Christmas has even gotten to her a bit, because she listens to Alex when he speaks without interrupting, even going so far as to look interested in what he has to say.

She also absentmindedly takes care of Jasper, who is in his high chair between her and Alex. Between words, she feeds him minuscule bites of pancakes, patting his mouth between each one. If I didn't know any better, I might think she had the potential to be a wonderful grandmother, except I'm almost positive that Margaret can never give up her scheming ways or be able to shirk her unending desire to be in control. Maybe there's something wrong with me, but I actually feel a small pang of sadness thinking of Jasmine and Jasper growing up without their only remaining grandmother, Alex's mom, but there is nothing I can do to change her heart or mind.

"This is almost enjoyable," my dad jokes, looking around the table at all of us. "It almost makes me sad that we're going home after tomorrow."

"It is sad," Catherine agrees. "But I'm sure we'll come back soon."

"Are you ready to get back to university?" Dad asks me before taking another bite of breakfast, waiting for my response.

I roll my eyes to the ceiling, taking a deep breath. "On one hand, yes, but on the other hand, I'm sort of panicking about school, the gallery, and the twins at the same time."

"It will be fine," he responds, no doubt in his voice. "You always persevere. Look at Matt, he has a very successful YouTube Channel and is a great student."

"I guess," I agree reluctantly.

My mind is swimming with thoughts of the upcoming months when Alex bumps me with his shoulder, knocking me from my reverie. I look up at him, a questioning look on my face.

"I have one more present," he tells me, keeping his voice quiet so only I can hear. "I wasn't sure if I was going to be able to get the reservation on Christmas day, but I got the confirmation this morning that we are booked."

"Not more skiing, right?" I ask, holding a hand to my chest. My legs and thighs are so utterly sore from yesterday that I think another ski trip might be the end of me.

"No, I swear," he says with a chuckle. "Something much more up your alley."

I fold my hands and wait, knowing he's wanting me to ask what it is, but I hold out, the corners of my mouth twitching until he sighs heavily, relenting and spilling his secret.

"It's a private hot spring. I've got us three hours, totally alone," his hand slides up my leg under the table as he speaks, "in one of the hottest, purest springs in Aspen."

I could moan out loud. It sounds so wonderful, but I keep my ecstatic noises to myself at the family breakfast table. Alex knows me all too well, and he's totally right. A hot spring IS right up my alley. Today, with my sore muscles, I can't think of anything that sounds better than a long soak.

And… whatever other mischief Alex and I may get up to in the spring. Or outside the spring. Or beneath the water. All I'm saying is that we can definitely find *something* to occupy our time in such a sultry setting.

Alex's hand is still creeping up my leg as he speaks, his fingers getting dangerously close to my inner thighs. "I've already told Mother that she's watching the kids again for a little while today, but since she's leaving tomorrow morning, I told her we'd be back within about six hours. How long will it take you to get ready?"

I look at him from under my lashes, loading all the sexiness I possibly can into my gaze. "I'll race you."

***

We packed a few things for the hot springs, but I think Alex and I both knew that we wouldn't need much, so with just a duffle bag full of towels and a change of clothes, we set out for our quick getaway.

The twins are exhausted from the excitement of opening all the gifts, and they're napping, arms stretched above their heads, in their playpens. I had expected that Dad and Catherine would have left by now, so I'm surprised to see Margaret and Catherine still sitting together in the living area, talking like old friends, with Dad nowhere to be found.

I shoulder my bag and look them over. "Where's my dad?"

Catherine waves a hand delicately, "He had to make a few calls, and frankly I'm bored to death sitting around and listening to him work, so I'm going to stay here and help with the children."

Great, I think with a scowl, as if Margaret watching them wasn't bad enough.

I shake off the uncomfortable feelings, determined to not let these two ruin my day. I'm going to have a delicious three hours at the hot springs, a wonderful Christmas dinner, and then tomorrow I will be back home. It will be lovely.

The sun is still shining brightly outside, and it takes my eyes a minute to adjust. I'm not surprised to see our SUV idling on the curb waiting for us, but what does surprise me is to see one of Alex's security agents in the front seat. I had thought he didn't bring any security detail to Aspen, and I can't say I'm happy to see this reminder of how strangely public and dangerous our lives can be.

"Why is this my first time seeing him?" I ask Alex as he opens the back seat door for me.

Alex rubs the back of his neck, and I know I will not like the answer he's about to give me. "Honestly, I had a few of them flown in before us. They're staying in the main portion of the hotel. I wasn't sure if we'd be spotted or not here and if any trouble popped up, I wanted to be prepared."

"So much for a quiet family Christmas," I mutter, buckling myself in. "No offense," I add, speaking to the driver.

"None taken, ma'am."

Alex climbs in from the other side and continues to explain his reasoning. "Iron Mountain Hot Springs are an hour or so away, and with us being that far from town, I didn't want us to be totally alone. Jamie here will wait in the SUV the whole time, though, so don't worry. It's still completely private, just you and me."

I jerk my head towards the back window, where a second black on black vehicle has pulled up and is idling behind ours. "And them?"

Alex groans, pinching the bridge of his nose as the driver pulls out onto the road, the second security vehicle following behind. "Okay, okay. I didn't lie about them having stayed on site, but the truth is, I've been having them watch the villa from the parking lot overnight, and last night there was someone skulking around the gardens. They took off before security could see who it was, and we're confident it was just a tourist that had drank a little too much, but I wanted security to accompany us today, so we are safe. So you are safe, Petra. I was hoping you'd never have to know they were here, but I can't say I'm not glad we have the option now."

My heartbeat kicks into high gear, thinking about someone outside of our villa while we were all sleeping, especially with my babies down the hall! "So we're taking security with us, but we're leaving Jasmine and Jasper without any!? We need to turn back, Alex."

He takes my hands between his, kissing my fingers. "Calm down, love. That's why Roy was gone when we came down. He was calling his security guys to post up outside."

That calms me down, but I roll my eyes when Alex's words sink in. "So you're saying Dad had secret security too?"

Alex laughs, a little self-conscious. "Well, you know. We are business partners for a reason. Great minds think alike, and all that."

"Paranoid minds, you mean." I relax, flipping on the heated seats. "But you both were right this time. I'm thankful."

"Thank you for trusting my judgement," Alex says, seemingly relieved that I'm not going to argue. "It would be an awkward three hours at this spring if you were pissed at me."

I nudge him a little with my arm. "I don't know about all that. We've had some pretty great anger sex before."

***

Iron Mountain Hot Springs is a sprawling resort, with dozens of pools scattered around the grounds, and the steam can be seen rising from the water all the way from the road. Alex makes a call, and we don't even have to get out of the car to check in. One employee comes out and checks the confirmation email Alex presents to them on his phone, and we're given an access card for one of the private springs behind the resort, made secluded by a stone fence and a wrought-iron gate that swings open for us with a swipe of the card.

Alex pulls up the map and frowns. "Security won't be able to see us from the parking lot, but they'll have a decent view of the area overall. Are you okay with that?"

I consider it for a moment. "Well, we can't exactly have them in the pool with us, so yes. That will be okay."

Decided, we grab our things and set out on foot for the private spring, located around the back side of a large boulder and over a small wooden footbridge. It isn't far at all, but it gives us just enough distance between the security cars and the spring for us to have full privacy.

The spring is the size of a small commercial pool, naturally fed from the underground hot spring, but made more accessible by the man-made cobblestone patio surrounding the pool and the gray stone tiles lining the inside of the basin. A few lounge chairs are present as well, but I have a feeling there won't be much lounging going on today.

I can feel the heat radiating off the water, and it's heavenly. It warms the area enough that I can already unzip my puffy coat, depositing it gently on the back of one of the lounge chairs. Even my cable-knit sweater feels a little bulky, but I don't want to seem too eager by getting naked immediately.

The spring is glorious, of course, but nothing can compare with the spectacular view. The Rockies jut into the sky like giants, snow-capped and blocking out the sky. About five feet from the spring, the warmth from the water dissipates, and the ground is once again blanketed in snow, making the hot spring feel like a small oasis in a frozen tundra.

I'm taking everything in, having set my bag down at my feet, when I feel Alex come close behind me and slip his hands under my sweater and up my bare back. I realize his arms are bare, and he's down to a white t-shirt and jeans already. When I glance down, his feet are bare, too.

"In a rush?" I ask him, shivering as his hands push under my bra, unclasping it and skating his hands over my back.

"To get inside with you, yes," he murmurs, his lips whispering over my jaw and the shell of my ear.

"Fine," I tell him, stepping away from his grasp and tugging my sweater over my head.

"Or after," he adds, watching me undress like a lion watching a gazelle. He unbuttons his jeans, pushing them to his feet and stepping out, all the while never taking his gaze off me.

It's distracting me, watching his taut, muscled body revealed, and my fingers fumble at the buttons of my own pants before they hit the ground, I shrug out of my already-unclasped bra and kick my boots far from me, and we're suddenly both in just our underwear, waiting for each other to make a move.

Even this close to the hot spring, the air chills me, and I wrap my arms around myself. "Brrr. Come on, I don't want to stand out here all day."

Alex raises a single eyebrow, seeming to be completely unaffected by the cold as he stalks, almost predatory, to the edge of the spring. I get a quick glance at the toned globes of his ass as she shucks his underwear, and then he's beneath the water, having dove gracefully in.

I follow, my skin covered in goosebumps, throwing my panties aside and sitting on the edge of the pool before sliding in, letting myself sink completely beneath the water and popping back out, slicking my long hair away from my face.

"Alex?" I call, looking around without seeing him, but then a pair of arms wraps around my middle. My husband nips my shoulder gently, growling in his throat.

I jump, squeaking out of surprise, before melting into his embrace. The water is just one step below too hot, and for the first time since landing in Aspen, I think I may be completely and totally warm all over.

Alex's body is firm behind me, but his skin is like velvet, and we both float, carefree, for a few long, blissful minutes.

The trance is broken when something hard and insistent presses into my lower back, and I giggle, rotating in his arms until we're facing each other, my arms looped around his neck and our faces inches apart.

"What did I say about relaxing first?" I admonish, but Alex's hands are supporting me by gripping my ass, and my voice comes out airier than intended.

"I'm relaxed," he insists. "And you are, too."

"I am?"

His lips move from my neck to my shoulders, and then to my chest as he leans me back in the water. I'm nearly floating on my back as he laps at the slopes of my breasts before taking my nipples, one by one, between his teeth in little love bites. I gasp, snaking my legs around him and pulling him closer.

"You are," he says again, tone thick with lust.

"Okay, I guess I am," I admit as he returns his mouth to my tits, causing bolts of pleasure to shoot from my chest to my core, liquid and molten.

His member is jutting against me, and I rotate my hips as much as I can, making the head slide through my folds and over my aching clit. I'm alive with arousal, urgent and bright. I've been waiting for this ever since Alex mentioned the spring, and now that we have arrived, I feel like I can't wait any longer.

Alex's hands slide from my ass to my back, sitting me back up and slanting his mouth over mine before his tongue darts in and my eyes flutter closed, kissing him back with a fervor that shocks me. Screw foreplay. I want him *now.*

I show him with my body, grinding against him as we kiss, until we are both panting from the lust building between us, but when I reach down to position him at my entrance, he stops me, a hand wrapped around my wrist.

"Not so fast," he growls. "You're going to come first."

I want to argue, I really do, but my mouth can't find the words to protest as he grips my hips in his hands and swims up to the edge of the spring, lifting me out until I'm perched on the edge, only my calves still submerged.

"Alex, I'm freezing," I object, finding it easier to speak now that I'm back in the frigid air.

"You won't be for long," he promises, pushing my knees apart until I'm on full display for him.

With a curse, he forgoes any build up, and before I can say anything else, his dark head is between my thighs, his mouth and fingers finding my most secret areas like a heat-seeking missile.

"Ohmygod," I choke out as his clever tongue circles my clit, his fingers delving deep within me. This isn't a slow, patient seduction. Alex wants me to come, and my God, I am going to, and fast.

He crooks his fingers in that magic come-hither gesture, changing the sparks of pleasure into an overwhelming wave that has me gasping for breath. When he ceases licking and wraps his lips around the pearl of my ecstasy, I feel the orgasm winding around my spine, set to explode.

Arms shaking, I collapse flat on my back on the stone right before the climax rips through me, and I cry my husband's name to the cloudless sky. But he doesn't give me time to rest. Instead, wrapping his hands around my hips and lifting me back into the water, even as I'm still spasming deep inside.

"What—?" I try to ask, light-headed, but my words evaporate into the air as he braces me against the back of the spring, pulling my legs around his waist and impaling me on his cock with one smooth stroke.

"Fuck," he grits out, giving us both time to adjust. I'm teetering on the edge of another climax from his sudden but welcome intrusion into my body, and I know I'm a goner when he starts moving.

But Alex surprises me, and instead of pushing in deep and fast, he makes love to me, slow and gentle, whispering words of affection into my ear as he feeds himself into me with agonizing slowness, over and over again. The water is shallow enough here that he can stand, and he makes it clear that he's in no rush now that he's inside of me.

Time stretches out, and I lose track of the minutes as they pass, surrendering myself body and soul to my husband.

We alternate between kissing and sharing honeyed words, wrapped up in each other as the world seems to fall away.

But eventually, I can feel the stutter in his thrusts, and I know he's reaching the end of his patience and control. His cock is thickening even more inside of me, which means his orgasm is on the horizon.

The knowledge brings that insatiable lust back to me tenfold, and I'm shocked when I hear myself begging, "Fuck me, Alex. Please fuck me." My body has taken control, and Alex growls fiercely at my commands.

"Hands on the edge, back to me," he snaps, and I scramble to comply. One of his hands is placed between my breasts, and the other grips my hip as he fits himself into me beneath the water, his manhood feeling even hotter inside of me than the surrounding spring.

Waves splash over the edge of the pool as he fucks me punishingly, taking what he needs from me, and all I can do is hold on. I can tell from the sounds of his breathing that he's close, but he's insistent on taking me over that edge with him, his hand sliding from my chest to where we are joined, working my clit expertly. The sensation makes everything else amplified to almost unbearable levels, and I don't even know myself what I'm asking of him as he bottoms out in me again and again.

I don't have any warning this time. One second he's pushing into me, and the next I'm coming, gripping his cock with my inner walls as my entire body is electrified, every one of my nerves coming alive. Once he feels my orgasm pulling him in deeper, Alex grunts once, and spills himself deep into my channel, fucking me through both of our climaxes.

My eyes are screwed shut as the flashes of pleasure begin to abate, and when I can finally open them again, I expect to see only the mountains and sky watching the end of our lovemaking silently.

What I don't expect is the figure, dressed all in black and hidden between two pines on the edge of the private spring area. And I *really* don't expect the flash of a camera coming from him either.

"Alex!" I shriek, all but kicking him off of me as I fling myself back into the water, my arms crossed hard around my chest to cover myself. I point a shaking finger at the paparazzi, who, seeing that we've taken notice, flees. "He was recording us!"

Alex says nothing, but his rage is instantaneous. He rockets from the water, but hesitates, nude, before chasing the other man down. He curses loudly, realizing he'll never catch up, instead digging his cell phone out of his bag and punching a number in before giving an order into the speaker. "There's someone here! A paparazzi or something! Catch him right the fuck now!"

***

I don't remember getting out of the pool or pulling my clothes onto my soaking body without even drying off. I can barely think as both Alex's security detail and Iron Mountain's own security send people to get our information while the rest of them search the grounds.

"I can't express how sorry I am," the manager of the resort says, with genuine sorrow in her voice. "We've never had *anything* like this happen here before."

"I don't want to fucking hear it," Alex snaps, wrapping a blanket around my shivering shoulders as I sit, hunched over, in one of the lounge chairs. "Just find that motherfucker, or you'll be hearing from my lawyer."

But they don't find him, even after putting the whole resort under severe scrutiny. Alex, vibrating with barely controlled anger, leads me back to the waiting SUV, our silent driver stiff in the front seat. I'm not sure who Alex blames the most: the Iron Mountain team, his own security, or himself.

We don't speak on the hour long drive back to the villa, but Alex is gentle and comforting, letting me lay my head on him as he makes call after call to try and get to the bottom of the horrible situation we have found ourselves in.

I sniffle, wiping tears from the corners of my eyes. The last thing I need is a video of Alex and I naked and fucking all over the web. I can already picture my dad deadly embarrassed and Margaret snickering at the whole thing. *Oh gosh, what a humiliation that would be.*

"Hey," Alex murmurs, holding his phone away from his face. "Don't cry, we'll get this taken care of."

I nod, but only to placate him. It's Christmas, for God's sake. Of course this would happen to me!

Alex calls everyone we know in the media, as well as our lawyer. That's the longest conversation of them all, going on for almost twenty minutes as Alex tries to build a legal fence around us before anything scandalous gets leaked.

I feel violated, like my whole body has been on display for the entire world to see. It makes me feel dirty and used. Worst of all, no one that Alex calls has any information about who the paparazzi could have been or who they may have been working for. Videos of public figures like us could sell, but not for as much as regular photos, since they can't be posted on mainstream sources. So why would someone want a video of us having sex?

It isn't until we arrive back at the villa, exhausted and heartsick, that the idea of the video being for revenge takes hold in my mind. Margaret is there to greet us and obviously knows that something fishy is going on. Our security and my dad's are on high alert, making themselves obvious instead of hidden, and I'm sure one of our mutual contacts has messaged or called her while we were gone.

She shoots up from where she's sitting, her hands clasped in front of her. "What is going on?"

I clamp my mouth shut. I will *not* humiliate myself by telling this witch that some random man recorded me while having sex with her son. She'll likely throw it in my face at the most opportune time. She always wants to have something to hold over my head.

As I come to think of it, the nebulous idea that Margaret could possibly be involved is swimming in my mind. Alex sighs heavily, sitting down in one chair and holding his head in his hands. To my utter shock, he opens his mouth and starts telling his mother everything I was trying to avoid her finding out.

"There was this guy," he starts. "At the spring, who started recording us while we were...well, I'm sure you can gather what we were doing."

I can only stare blankly in horror as he shares everything. Margaret simply nods, pulling out her phone mid-conversation and tapping on it periodically as she continues to listen, until Alex is finished laying our shame bare.

I get up, turning my back to them both, planning on taking a hot shower where I can bawl my eyes out in peace. Margaret ignores me, but I can feel Alex's eyes on my back as I retreat. Right before I'm out of earshot, I hear Margaret tell Alex, "Let me handle this, my son. I'll make it go away."

***

Dinner is a blur, too. Everything is muted and subdued, including the energy of everyone at the table. My dad looks almost as furious as Alex, his jaw clenched hard enough that it's visible from across the table. Margaret is absent, but I pay it no mind. I simply feed my children, take them upstairs to bathe, and lay them down for sleep.

Christmas ends on a much darker note than I could have ever imagined, and when Alex lays next to me that night, a million things run through my mind. I want to rage at him for telling Margaret, cry about how the spring was supposed to be a safe place for us and mourn how our perfect Christmas trip had turned out in the end.

Instead, I scoot over to him, folding myself into his arms and letting him wordlessly stroke my back and whisper reassurances into my hair.

I don't think that I will be able to sleep, but the emotional toll of the day has worn me to the bone, and after some time in my husband's comforting embrace, I drift off, sleeping fitfully.

CHAPTER 8

Aspen, December 26, 2021
Petra Van Gatt

"Petra, Alex," Margaret says brightly as Alex and I descend the stairs the next morning, a baby in each of our arms. Her white hair is pulled tightly back from her face and her make-up impeccably done.

We're dressed like we're getting ready for breakfast, but Margaret looks ready to lord over a business brunch, even though I know she's flying home today. Her positivity unsettles me, and my chest still feels hollowed out from the day before.

"Yes, Mom?" Alex asks distractedly, accepting the bottle that Earl the butler hands him. "What is it?"

"Your little situation," Margaret emphasizes her words, wiggling her fingers as if brushing something off. "It's taken care of. Finished. Don't give it a second thought."

Both Alex and I pause, freezing in place. "What?" I ask lamely.

"What exactly do you mean?" Alex elaborates.

"I told you I would handle it, and I did," Margaret says vaguely. "If any video emerges on the web, the people I have contacted will take it down immediately."

I say nothing else, lost in thought, as I feed Jasmine her breakfast. I'm obviously relieved, but I hate thinking that Margaret is the cause of my relief. Owing Margaret something means that she will lord the debt to her over your head for years, using it to manipulate anything and everything to get the outcome she wants.

I think of Emma and Yara, and how their affair is the only bargaining chip I've ever held over Margaret all this time. First, I had thought Margaret hired Catherine to slowly wring secrets from my father and use them to control me, but now it seems to make just as much sense that she hired the paparazzi herself to either shame me, or so she could be the hero and once again leave me in her debt.

Or, even worse, she could have done both. It seems like something Margaret would do, leaving no stone unturned for revenge. It eats at me all morning, even as I watch the tension flow away from Alex and gratitude to his mother replace it. I find it odd that my meticulous shark of a husband wouldn't demand more information, but… I guess he has a blind spot with his mother.

I work all morning on a text message to Emma, explaining everything that had happened, wanting to both warn her and get her opinion, but so much has happened that I haven't finished it by the time Earl is getting the car ready for Margaret to leave. When suddenly I hear a few knocks on the door of our bedroom, and as I shout to come in, I'm shocked to see it's Margaret herself coming over.

"Petra," she says, her tone unusually sweet. "My driver is here. Would you… mind accompanying me to the airport? I'd love to talk to you; just the two of us."

I swallow hard at her question. What does she want to talk about? Holy shit…

"Of course," I mumble, before standing up and heading outside with her.

As I reach the foyer, my eyes stumble on Alex and then on my dad and Catherine who have come over to our villa to tell her goodbye.

I watch her hug Alex, and then kiss my children on their chubby cheeks, all the while seeing flashes in my mind of the paparazzi in the pines and Catherine whispering in her ear. My heart is in my throat as I tell Alex discretely that I'm going with Margaret to the airport. He nods, most likely knowing it already.

"Be careful," he whispers, before giving me a quick hug.

Margaret and I leave the villa, heading towards the car which is parked in front. We sit in the back, and a cold silence emerges when we shut our respective doors.

No one dares to talk despite the quiet music playing in the background. I remain tense, watching out of the window at the passing landscape as the driver takes us away.

"It was a lovely Christmas," Margaret comments, breaking the silence between us. "Thank you for having me."

I give her a smile in return, not knowing what to reply back. I'm not a confrontational person, but I can't hold it in anymore. After these four long days biting my tongue, I'm more than ready to make myself known. "Did you know about Catherine before my dad's introduction?"

Margaret doesn't seem much surprised by my question. "I know her," she says vaguely. "But she changed quite a lot since her divorce from Paul."

"You mean physically?" I ask.

"Yes," Margaret answers, putting on a plastered smile. "She didn't used to be blonde before, or so thin."

"How did you know her?" I keep asking.

"Oh, she used to be a close friend of Julia," she answers, confirming exactly what I already knew. I'm surprised that she isn't even hiding the truth. "Then there was a messy divorce, and she disappeared from the public eye for a while."

"Do you know who introduced her to my dad?"

Margaret looks in my direction, amused at my constant curiosity. "I do not." For some reason, it feels like she's lying shamelessly to my face.

The rest of the drive goes by silently. And as the driver reaches the airport, I wonder why on earth she wanted me to come with her since I was the one doing all the talking.

When we get to the tarmac, the driver stops in front of the jet, and a staff member opens our respective doors. Her plane seems to be ready, so I go around the car and get ready to tell her goodbye. Still, I'm tactful, leaning close to her so I can be heard over the plane's engines.

"Thank you for taking care of the paparazzi situation, Margaret. I know planning that entire ordeal couldn't have been easy."

She smiles at me, a predatory showing of teeth that reminds me of her son. "It was nothing." She reaches out to grip my upper arm, her sharp nails pressing through my coat and into my arm. "But, there is something I'll ask of you in repayment."

Margaret doesn't ask for the favor, she simply lets me know I'll be doing it for her. "What?" I snap.

"It's nothing, really. You may even enjoy it." The older woman takes a deep breath, and I realize whatever she's about to tell me is distasteful to her. "My lovely Yara has a polo tournament in St. Moritz next month, and I've caught wind that she will, unfortunately, be bringing your little friend *Emma* with her." Margaret basically spits my best friend's name, and hearing it on her lips causes my stomach to tighten. "This nasty affair has got to end, Petra."

"It's up to them to decide," I riposte.

"Oh, no, it's not," she answers just as fast. "The last thing I need is this whole thing to blow up in the news. So you'll accompany your little friend to St. Moritz, and you'll make sure that she puts an end to it once and for all."

"I can't do that!" I exclaim. Emma is going to be furious, and I'm still reeling trying to figure out how Margaret has found out about Yara inviting Emma when I haven't even heard of my friend going to St. Moritz yet. Did she hire the paparazzi just to manipulate me to do this favor for her?

"Oh, of course you can, dear," she pulls me in closer still, telling me quietly with an acid tone. "And you will, or you'll regret it, Petra. I promise you that."

Bizarrely, she kisses my cheeks, holding on to my shoulders. I'm too shocked to shove her away, and by the time she's finished, she's pulling her enormous sunglasses over her eyes and giving me a jaunty little finger wave.

"Goodbye, dear. Thanks again for going to St. Moritz for me," Margaret says as she makes her way to the plane. She climbs the stairs of her own jet and is beyond my sight, leaving me alone to deal with the bomb she has just dropped.

I'm left standing on the tarmac behind the car, a hand pressed to my cheek where Margaret had kissed me goodbye. I'm not sure if it's an overreaction, but it almost seems to burn.

CHAPTER 9

Aspen, December 26, 2021
Petra Van Gatt

On my way back home, I remain both shocked and confused at Margaret's request. How can she have the guts to threaten me like that? What a psycho she is… Well, now it's clear that she is linked to the guy who recorded us. Maybe she is even the one who asked him to go and do that. Who knows? But one thing is sure; she must have access to that video to threaten me so shamelessly. She has nothing else against me if not for the video. No matter what she does with it, I can't go to St. Moritz and ask my best friend to break up with her lover. That's totally inappropriate! I mean, Emma will never agree to it. Heck, even me, I will never have the audacity to ask my friend to do something like that. Despite not liking their relationship one tiny bit, it's none of my business. I lean my head back on the headrest and heave a long sigh, still processing what just happened a few minutes ago.

So this is why Margaret came here? To find a way to get me to comply with her request? I wish I could think otherwise, but it's just too obvious that the whole sweet and caring grandmother thing was all bullshit. And what would happen if I don't comply? What if I just stay in Manhattan instead? Is she gonna release that video for the whole world to see?

"Miss?" the driver says, pulling me back to planet Earth. "You can get out, if you're ready. We've arrived."

I look out of the window, and notice the car has already stopped and is parked in the underground garage of the villa. I thank him and step outside, my mind still ruminating on Margaret's request. I take the stairs, heading to the first floor, and as I open the door that leads to the foyer, I'm smashed by the strong heat coming from the fireplace. I take off my coat immediately, followed by my boots, and hearing footsteps approaching, my eyes drift up to meet with Alex's intriguing face.

"Everything alright?" he asks.

I cock my head to the side, unable to answer him positively. Should I tell him the truth? Like the *whole* truth? I heave a long sigh, undecided.

"Uh-oh," Alex utters, most likely reading me like an open book. "Something happened, huh?"

"Yeah," I say pensively. Then giving a glance around the open floor, I ask, "Are we alone?"

"Yep!" There's a trace of a smile lingering on his lips. "The twins are sleeping and your dad is spending the day with Catherine."

"Good," I answer mechanically, my thoughts drifting to Margaret again. Not knowing how to start, I make my way towards the living area of the villa, more specifically to where the fireplace is burning brightly, heating up the entire floor, and Alex follows me closely behind in silence.

As I stand in front of the burning logs, warming up my hands, he says, "What happened? You look worried."

He knows me well. While I try to remain unbothered, what happened has left a bitter taste in my mouth and I don't think I can pretend any longer. "Well," I begin, carefully choosing my words since, no matter what, Margaret is still Alex's mom. "Your mom wants me to do something for her that I simply cannot bring myself to do."

I turn to check his reaction, but he's just stoically looking at me. "Like what?"

I release a long breath, my heart tightening as I recall what she asked me to do. "She wants me to go to St. Moritz and ask Emma to break up with Yara."

His eyes widen immediately in surprise, and his mouth literally drops. "How come she knows about them?"

"Because I told her at the baptism," I disclose, my eyes drifting away for a moment. "And I also said I'd go and tell Elliot if she doesn't leave us alone."

Alex runs a hand through his hair, processing everything I just told him. "Holy shit," he blurts out. "And what if you don't do what she asked you?"

"Well, she said I will regret it," I fess up.

"What!" All of a sudden, Alex shoves his hand in the back pocket of his jeans, pulling his iPhone out. "I'm gonna call her the fuck now." He then storms to the dining room and roams around as if he's trying to cool himself down.

I follow him and stand still as I observed his distress. "Alex—"

"No!" he snaps, nearly barking. "She really crossed the line this time." I'm glad to know his anger is directed to his mom but I wonder how she will react knowing I told him everything. He finishes typing on the screen and brings the phone up to his ear.

I look at him from the living room while he stands by the dining table, a hand on his hips. He exhales loudly, his frustration truly palpable, as we both wait for his mom to pick up the call.

Maybe she's already asleep in the plane, I think to myself.

"Hi, Mom, how are you doing?" I hear him finally saying, his tone stern and steady, but not aggressive. He nods as she speaks, but then the more he listens, the more confused he seems to be. "What are you talking about?" he asks, before starting to stroll around the dining area, a hand shoved in one of the back pockets of his jeans. My heartbeat keeps thundering anxiously fast as I observe him pacing around. Oh gosh, what are they talking about? Alex remains silent while listening to her speaking. Unfortunately, he isn't on speaker so I can only imagine what she is telling him. Is she talking about me? Who knows what Margaret is capable of! "This is none of our business!" Alex spits out. "She doesn't have to do shit!" I heave a long sigh, walking towards him—he seems way tenser than before. "Why are you doing this?" He stops and stands still, his back on me. He then runs a hand through his hair, and it feels like Alex is completely lost. "I'm gonna speak to her." He finally turns around, the phone still against his ear, but his eyes are on me—and they are quite serious. "Alright, I get it," he nearly grits between teeth. "Goodbye." And he hangs up, anger laced all over his face.

"What happened?"

A gush of air rolls off his lips, his chest rising and falling as he does so. "She said you either persuade Emma to end the affair or she'll tell Elliot herself and he'll ask Yara to take care of it."

"What?" I blink twice, totally speechless for a moment as I process what he just said. "Take care of it? I can't believe it!" I shut my eyes as if I was trying to wake up from the nightmare I put myself in. If only I'd have kept my mouth shut at the cathedral! Damn it! "That doesn't make sense! Why would she tell him though?" I ask in confusion. "Your mom is bluffing!"

"As you might understand, Mom doesn't like covering up affairs." He pauses, taking a deep breath in and out. "I think she is telling the truth."

No, she is definitely lying. If I don't comply, what she will do is release that video on the web, but of course she is not gonna tell her precious son that she owns a copy. While she didn't admit it to my face either, I'm pretty sure she has one! But if what she's saying is true though, Emma will never forgive me. Of course Yara will drop Emma like yesterday's news if Elliot makes her an ultimatum. And Emma will blame me for the whole thing since she knows I shared her secret with Margaret. *Holy shit…*

"Emma needs to find intimacy and romance somewhere else," Alex announces, a mix of sadness and gravity in his tone.

"Well, yeah, that I know," I answer back.

"No, I mean, what if we set her up with someone? Someone who is single, of course."

"Oh," I utter in shock. I wasn't ready for such a question, and I must say it sounds totally crazy to me.

Alex, on the other hand, seems to be ruminating further about this possibility. "Someone like my sister, but single…"

"And what if it doesn't work?" I interpose immediately. "Like, I think she is really in love with Yara."

"Yeah, after so many months, I figured she'd be quite attached to her." His eyes drift down to the floor and Alex seems totally engrossed in his own thoughts. "Maybe some edgy artist or sportswoman that lives in Manhattan."

I shake my head at him. "You don't understand. Emma and Yara are quite similar; they are both rich and spoiled, they enjoy the same type of sports, and seem to have a very, um, peculiar dynamic." At least I hadn't told anyone about the naked portrait I made for them. "Anyone else compared to her, will feel bland and uninteresting."

"If Emma doesn't break up with her, Yara will do it as soon as Elliot knows," Alex tells me, and it doesn't seem like he's joking. "And then Emma will be seriously mad at you."

"Emma will be mad at me just the same if I ask her to break up," I tell him straight away.

"Unless she meets someone else and loses interest in Yara," he circles back.

While I hate forcing fate on anyone, at the end of the day, Alex might be onto something. If only Emma could find someone else and drop Yara willingly. Is there really someone out there for her? Someone as interesting as Yara? Well, I guess there is only one way to find out…

CHAPTER 10

Aspen, December 27, 2021
Petra Van Gatt

Despite being overly tired, my thoughts have kept me awake the whole night. The last thing I want is to be responsible for Emma and Yara's break up but I'm not seeing how I can escape Margaret's request. If I don't comply, she will do it herself and Emma will inevitably know it was my fault. I heave a long sigh, my eyes feeling heavy as I try once more to fall asleep. A few minutes pass by, and since I'm still wide awake, I decide to observe my husband who lies beside me, peacefully snoozing on his pillow. I wish I could just switch off and do the same, but alas, I have to come up with a plan. In my opinion, Alex's idea of finding Emma another lover is nothing more than idealistic and near to impossible to achieve. Maybe I should just call her and tell her the whole truth. She would get pissed off, maybe stop talking to me for a few days, but ultimately, she would forgive me. I mean, her affair can't be more important than our friendship, right?

I take some deep breaths in and out, and check the clock on the nightstand once more: 5 a.m. Damn. I guess I should really get some sleep if I want to be a functioning adult and not a zombie during the day.

Sunlight seems to be casting through the window as I feel something beaming on my face. It's warm in here, way too warm. I pull down the sheets, my eyes slowly opening so they can get used to the strong sunlight that fills the room. I look beside me and find nothing but emptiness. Alex must have gotten up early. Then I check the clock and—

Jeez! Midday?!

I jump out of bed, baffled at how late it is! No wonder it's so bright in here. I rush to the bathroom, and take a quick shower to get ready for the day. Since Margaret already left, I decide to wear something more casual, a sweater and a pair of jeans would do. Once I'm done, I leave the room, cross the hallway, but stop in my tracks as I find Alex sitting at the dining table with his open laptop in front of him and a few sheets of paper spread on the table. *Is he already back to working mode?*

I get closer to him, and after giving a quick look at the papers, I notice all of them are resumés of female candidates with their photos printed out. Except all women seem quite young, attractive, and… they look super similar to Yara!

I take the first sheet I find, and read it through. "What is this?" I ask immediately, since it doesn't look like a proper CV for a job position.

"Good morning to you too," Alex answers instead, his tone cheeky. His eyes travel up to meet mine and, damn it, his smile is so beautiful that I can't help but feel all giddy at the sight of it. But I refocus on the present moment, and cock my head to the side in response, shooting him an impatient glare. "I have reached a few agencies that normally help with finding the perfect match," he explains, before handing me another stack of papers. "These are some of the profiles they sent me that are in theory a good fit for Emma."

"Alex," I say as I go around the table and stand beside him. He turns his body towards me, and I put my hands on his shoulders so that I can have his full attention. "There's no need for any of that. I'm going to talk to Emma and tell her the truth," I disclose. "She might get pissed off initially but I'm sure she will understand and talk to Yara."

While I thought Alex would be happy with my decision, his facial expression says otherwise. "Wait—you seriously think Emma will break up with my sister because you tell her to?" He sounds genuinely skeptical about it, but I'm quite positive of it.

"I have to try...."

He huffs, shaking his head in denial. "Petra, you are just wasting your time."

"I'll call her now," I tell him decidedly. "The sooner we know, the better." Before I start walking away though, I ask, "How are the twins?"

"They are good. I fed them this morning, then played a bit with them, and they are having a nap now."

A quick smile settles on my lips as I picture Alex doing all of that. I should take more pictures of him with the twins. I don't think I've taken enough of them since we arrived.

"Alright, I'll call her now before they wake up."

"Good luck," he mutters, before his attention returns to his laptop.

I take my iPhone and head back to our bedroom to make the phone call. There, I close the door behind me, and press the *call* button. The ringtone goes on, and on, and on…

"Hey!" Emma shouts from the other side of the line. "How was Christmas? Did you have a good time?"

"Hi Emma," I answer, and for some reason, I can't match her joyful tone. "It was great, Alex took me to a romantic getaway after lunch and it was wonderful. How was yours?" I ask as I try to relax for what is yet to come.

"It was good too," she says, not wanting to dwell in further details. "What about Margaret? Is she still there?"

"No, she left yesterday actually," I tell her.

"Oh, that's great," she comments. "So she was just there for Christmas and that's it? No drama?" Oh boy, the question she just made. I wonder whether or not I should tell her about the paparazzi. But after some reflection, I decide not to. "Is everything okay?" she asks after a moment, since I'm not answering.

"Um, well, it's a bit complicated," I finally fess up.

"What do you mean?"

I keep quiet for a moment, my heartbeat rising anxiously fast at what I'm about to say. I have no idea how to start the subject matter, so I start with a simple question. "Are you and Yara still together?"

"That question again?"

"It's just..." I pause, trying to find the best words to put on. "Margaret wants it to end."

"That's not my problem," she shoots back. And, truthfully, I wasn't expecting any other reaction.

"Well, she is ready to go and talk to Elliot if you don't break up first." And she might also publish a very graphic video of me and her son on the web, but I refrain myself from telling her that.

"I'm not gonna break up with her," Emma answers straight away. "If she wants to talk to him, then good luck."

My brows raise up, surprised at how relaxed she seems to be. "You really want to test her?"

"I'm not afraid of her," she snaps. "Like zero percent."

"What if she does talk to Elliot, and he asks his wife to break up with you?"

"He'll never do that."

"Why not?" I ask, still confused at her confidence.

"Because it makes his wife happy so I'm sure whatever makes her happy, Elliot will be okay with." I don't know much about Elliot, but I'm pretty sure Emma is very misguided. Does she really believe Elliot is gonna be okay with his wife's affair being all over the news while he knew nothing about it?

"How can you be so sure?" I ask her, genuinely concerned at her naivety. "Do you know if Yara said anything to him about you?"

Emma doesn't answer immediately. She blows out a loud breath instead, pondering my question a bit further. "I don't know if she did," she says a bit coyly. "But I know they mean a lot to each other."

"Emma," I begin, my tone more poised than before. "Elliot will most likely give her an ultimatum if he knows about you. And I don't think Yara will hesitate to make a choice."

Silence settles in now that Emma finally understands that this affair was meant to end. "Why did you have to tell Margaret about us, huh?" Her aggressiveness catches me off guard and I wonder what I'm supposed to reply to that. "My relationship with Yara was none of your damn business!" Her tone keeps rising, but I know she's just hurt at the eventuality she might lost Yara once and for all. "I think we had agreed not to talk about it, no?"

"Yes, but—"

"Look," she says assertively, cutting me off. "I've always been super supportive with you. But now I need you to do the same and to stop interfering." Poor Emma. Doesn't she understand that it's only a matter of time until Elliot knows the truth? "Now I have to go. Goodbye."

"Emma, wait!"

Despite my request, Emma just hangs up on me.

I guess Alex was right—talking to her was pointless. And now she might even go and tell Yara about our little phone call.

Great.

I heave a long sigh, disappointed at myself for being the reason they will ultimately break up. I can only hope Emma will forgive me.

I unlock the door and stroll slowly in the direction of the dining table where Alex is still reviewing the candidates.

"How was it?" I hear him asking.

I look up at him, his eyes filled with curiosity as he waits for me to tell him all the gritty details. "You were right. She basically told me to fuck off but in a more polite way."

Alex throws me a candid smile in return. "She is not gonna do it, huh?"

"Nope," I confirm, pacing towards him. "And I bet she is gonna tell Yara about our conversation."

"My plan doesn't sound so stupid now, does it?"

I exhale louder than usual, unable to deny it or admit it. "The thing is your mom wants me to go to St. Moritz to persuade Emma to break up with Yara," I tell him. "I don't even know why she wants me there."

"Most likely because reporters are gonna be on the hunt for some juicy content," Alex discloses, looking at me from behind his laptop. "And my sister is quite known for giving them exactly what they want."

I frown at his observation. "What do you mean?" As I keep observing him, his eyes drop to his screen and it seems like he's trying to ignore my question by typing something on his keyboard.

"Alex?" I stand tall in front of him, crossing my arms over my chest as I wait patiently for him to answer me.

He heaves a long sigh, leaning back on his chair. "Well, let's say there's always some sort of controversy surrounding her. That's it." And his attention returns to his screen where he resumes typing.

"What kind of controversy?" I press.

"Nothing," he utters briefly, keeping his eyes on the screen as he keeps typing on the keyboard.

"Tell me," I insist.

Since Alex knows I'm not gonna go anywhere, he blows out a breath in displeasure and says, "Look, my sister's life is none of my business, okay? I was just trying to help you out."

"What kind of controversy were you talking about?" My gaze follows his, and despite knowing he'd rather avoid this conversation, there's no escaping it.

"Fine," he hisses. "Emma is not her first girlfriend attending her tournament in St. Moritz," he discloses. And I'm not sure why, but I'm not surprised by his revelation. "A few years ago there were some articles claiming Yara was with another young girl. Mom did her best to silence those claims, but the media knows that every year in St. Moritz, Yara attends parties and flirts with much younger women. They just love to catch her on camera doing all kind of stuff. There was nothing that would lead to Elliot taking those gossips seriously, but this time might be different."

"Even if I tell Emma about those previous young girls, I bet she won't give a damn," I point out, my tone laced with disappointment. "She's simply too obsessed with her." As I come to think of it, maybe Alex's plan isn't that bad. Maybe we should focus our energy on finding someone that could make Emma forget Yara once and for all. I walk around the table, gathering the rest of the sheets from the table, and give a more attentive look at our potential candidates. Some women look exactly like Yara—fit, tall, dark brown eyes, pale skin, stern face—but what about their personalities? Are they the same too?

"We can schedule a face-to-face meet up with them, you know," Alex suggests as if he were listening to my own thoughts.

I don't reply immediately; I'm still assessing his plan: on one hand, if Emma falls in love with someone else, she'd drop Yara willingly without Elliot or Margaret getting involved or our little video going public. On the other hand though, finding someone that Emma could fall in love with to the point of forgetting Yara is almost impossible.

"Fine," I tell him, accepting the challenge. "Let's first check all candidates, and do a pre-selection screening before booking a Zoom call with them." I drag a chair to sit beside him and start studying the social media profile of each candidate.

"So, you are in?" Alex asks, visibly surprised.

"Well, if I can find the perfect woman for my best friend, someone who can genuinely love her and not use her like your sister does, then I guess I am."